"I hate what's happening, but I'm glad you're here. I don't think I could get through this without you."

Oh, man. That gave him a punch of emotion. Not of their usual heat, but of the feelings that he'd failed to protect her six months ago, and he couldn't fail her and Evan again.

He stood, pulling Hanna into arms and brushing one of those chaste—and hopefully comforting—kisses on the top of her head. She didn't melt against him this time though. She stayed a little stiff when she looked up at him. It seemed to Jesse that she had something to say. What exactly, he didn't know, but she didn't speak.

She kissed him instead.

Her mouth came to his, not some tentative, testing the waters gesture.

But holding back nothing.

TARGETED IN SILVER CREEK

USA TODAY Bestselling Author

DELORES FOSSEN

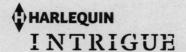

HARLEQUIN
INTRIGUE

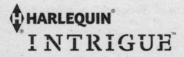

ISBN-13: 978-1-335-58270-6

Targeted in Silver Creek

Copyright © 2023 by Delores Fossen

Recycling programs
for this product may
not exist in your area.

For questions and comments about the quality of this book,
please contact us at CustomerService@Harlequin.com.

Harlequin Enterprises ULC
22 Adelaide St. West, 41st Floor
Toronto, Ontario M5H 4E3, Canada
www.Harlequin.com

Printed in U.S.A.

Delores Fossen, a *USA TODAY* bestselling author, has written over one hundred novels, with millions of copies of her books in print worldwide. She's received a Booksellers' Best Award and an RT Reviewers' Choice Best Book Award. She was also a finalist for a prestigious RITA® Award. You can contact the author through her website at www.deloresfossen.com.

Books by Delores Fossen

Harlequin Intrigue

Silver Creek Lawmen: Second Generation

Targeted in Silver Creek

The Law in Lubbock County

Sheriff in the Saddle
Maverick Justice
Lawman to the Core
Spurred to Justice

Mercy Ridge Lawmen

Her Child to Protect
Safeguarding the Surrogate
Targeting the Deputy
Pursued by the Sheriff

Visit the Author Profile page at Harlequin.com.

CAST OF CHARACTERS

Deputy Jesse Ryland—This Silver Creek lawman intends to protect his ex and his six-month-old son from an escaped prisoner.

Hanna Kendrick—Six months ago, a shooting robbed her of her memory, but she can still feel the heated attraction between her and Jesse...she's just not sure if she can trust him.

Evan Ryland—Jesse and Hanna's infant son. Even though he's not in the path of a killer, he could still be in danger.

Isabel Kendrick—Hanna's mother who has bad blood with the Ryland family, including Jesse. It's no secret that she doesn't want Hanna and Evan with Jesse.

Bullock "Bull" Freeman—On the surface, it seems as if he's a dangerous escaped con with an agenda of revenge, but maybe there's a different reason for his escape.

Agent Ryan Shaw—The ATF agent who's hunting for Bull and the leader of a criminal operation that's going on in Silver Creek.

Marlene Freeman—Bull's socialite sister who is seemingly an innocent bystander in an attack, but she could know a whole lot more than she's saying.

Chapter One

Deputy Jesse Ryland slid his hand over the Smith & Wesson in his holster. Normally, that wasn't something he'd do when paying a visit to Hanna Kendrick, but there was nothing normal about this evening.

Not with a killer on the loose.

A killer who might at this very second be making his way to Hanna.

Jesse couldn't rein in the motherlode of flashbacks that the killer's escape from prison was giving him because he knew just how serious a situation this was. As serious as it got for both the job and his personal life.

He'd been a deputy for nearly eight years now in Hanna's and his hometown of Silver Creek, Texas. Eight years of the badge in a family of badges. Being a cop was in his blood, and in those eight years he'd honed some instincts. Ones that had saved his life. And sometimes they'd let him down.

But he couldn't allow his instincts to fail him now.

Jesse made his way up the steps of the porch that stretched across the entire front of the pale yellow one-story house. It was a familiar trek for him since he came here at least four times a week to see his six-month-old son, Evan. Those visits with his little boy were priceless, but Hanna hadn't exactly made him feel welcome here. She wouldn't now either, and it didn't take long for Jesse to get confirmation of just that.

Hanna had obviously seen or heard him pull up because she unlocked and opened the door before Jesse could even knock. Even though it was fairly early, she'd already called it a night since she was wearing comfy purple PJs and had her long blond hair loose on her shoulders instead of scooped back in her usual ponytail.

Jesse caught the scent of lemon tea. And Hanna. Nothing flowery or from a bottle. Just her.

As usual, there was wariness in her deep green eyes, and she automatically stepped back as if to make sure they didn't accidentally touch or breathe in the same air. Not because she hated him. At least, Jesse didn't think she did anyway. But it was more of her not trusting him. Or anybody else for that matter.

The thin scar on the left side of her forehead had plenty to do with that.

A scar that caused even more flashbacks and bad memories for Jesse than a killer's escape had. Because that scar was a reminder of just how close she'd come to dying. When she'd been nine months pregnant with their son, no less. Evan and she had survived, thank God, but Hanna had paid a heavy price.

They all had.

"Jesse," she murmured on a rise of breath.

He heard the wariness that was always there but, as usual, Jesse saw something else. The glimmer of the heat between them. The same heat that had brought about the one-night stand resulting in her getting pregnant with Evan.

Of course, Hanna immediately concealed that glimmer by dodging his gaze. Again, that was the norm. She didn't want to feel heat for a man she didn't trust. A man she didn't even remember.

Hanna was holding her phone, and Jesse could see the app was still open for her security system. She would have had to disarm it before opening the door or it would have triggered the alarms, but he had no doubts that it had been armed when he'd arrived. There was no feeling of a safety net for her anymore, no carefree attitude. She structured her life around locks and security systems.

"Evan's already asleep," she added as that breath fell away. Hanna picked up the baby monitor from the foyer table where she'd likely set it when she had opened the door and showed him the image of the baby in his crib.

He nodded. Jesse knew his son's schedules and routines, and since it was going on eight thirty, Hanna would have already bathed Evan and put him down for the night.

"We need to talk," Jesse said.

She opened her mouth, closed it and then looked at him as if trying to suss out what this was all about.

It definitely wasn't the norm for him to come to her place when he hadn't arranged a visit with Evan.

"If this is about my amnesia, it hasn't gone away," Hanna volunteered. She absently touched the scar, the evidence of the gunshot wound that had robbed her of the memories of the attack.

And of Jesse.

As far as Hanna was concerned, she didn't recall a thing about meeting him. Or having sex with him. Didn't remember even a second of the bond they'd built when she'd been pregnant. Of course, it wasn't a strong enough bond for Hanna to marry him. Or to fall in love with him. But there sure as heck hadn't been this distance and mistrust that was there now.

"Did something happen to my mom?" she asked with some fresh alarm straining the muscles in her face.

"No," he assured her. "As far as I know, your mother is fine. It's about Bull Freeman."

Hanna's eyes widened and, while dragging in a hard breath, she dropped back another step. She might not have any actual memories of Bullock "Bull" Freeman shooting her in what had been a botched attempt to evade arrest, but Hanna was well aware that the man was behind bars.

Or rather that's where he should be.

A place he should have stayed until his upcoming trial since Bull hadn't been let out on bail.

"They let him out of jail?" she murmured.

Jesse shook his head and glanced behind him and around the yard. "He escaped."

He gave her a couple of seconds to let that sink in. Of course, it would take a lot longer than that for her to deal with it, but this was a start. There were lots of steps that needed to happen now.

Because the sweltering summer sun had finally set, making it next to impossible for Jesse to see if Bull was anywhere near the house, he took hold of Hanna's arm. Keeping his touch light and brief, he eased her backward so he could step inside and shut the door. He locked it and then motioned toward her phone that she was now holding in a death grip.

"Use your app to turn the security system back on," Jesse instructed, knowing it was going to give her another mental jolt.

It did. Her fingers were trembling when she did as he'd said. But she didn't stop there.

"Evan," she breathed, and she turned and started running down the hall in the direction of the nursery. Her bare feet sounded out in quick, soft thuds on the hardwood floors.

Jesse followed her while he glanced around the living room, taking particular notice of the windows. As usual, they were all shut, and Hanna had all the blinds fully lowered. That was routine for her now, but before she'd been shot and had her life turned upside down, those blinds had usually been open. No doubt so she could see the amazing views on the five acres of her property.

The house and the land had been in Hanna's family for several generations. An old money kind of place that managed to look both important and welcoming

at the same time. A hard thing to accomplish, which
was probably why Hanna had chosen to live here after
her late father had left her the property when she'd
barely been twenty. This was her home in every sense
of the word, which meant it was Evan's home as well.

The main area had an open floor plan, so it was
easy for him to take in the living room, dining room
and kitchen with only a couple of sweeping glances.
After Jesse had finished checking to make sure all the
windows in this part of the house were locked—they
were—he went down the hall, tracing her steps, and
he found Hanna standing over Evan's crib.

The room was dark except for a smattering of
milky-colored stars on the ceiling from the machine
pumping out the soothing sounds of a gentle rain. All
very serene. The perfect place for a baby to sleep.

Jesse went closer, moving shoulder to shoulder
with her while looking down at their son, and got
the same slam of emotion he always did when he saw
that precious little face. The love. The fierce need to
make him happy and keep him safe.

Evan's hair was nearly identical in color to Jesse's
own dark brown. So were his son's eyes, though Jesse
couldn't see them now because Evan was sacked out.
He certainly made a precious picture lying there.

When Jesse had been younger, he'd vowed he
would never have children, but that had all changed
with Evan. The love had been instant and solid. Of
course, that love only reminded him of just how much
was at stake right now. If Bull wanted to get back at

him in the worst possible way, then going after Evan would be the way to do it.

And Jesse wasn't going to let that happen.

"When? How?" Hanna asked in a whisper.

There was no need for her to clarify her questions, and Jesse was ready with the answers. "Bull escaped this afternoon. I didn't get the call, though, until about twenty minutes ago."

That'd felt like a gut punch, and Jesse's first instincts had been to call Hanna to tell her to lock up. But since he'd known she would have already done that, he had decided this was news best delivered in person. Especially since he was going to do much more than just play messenger tonight.

"According to the prison official who called the sheriff's office," Jesse went on, keeping his voice at a whisper so he wouldn't wake up Evan, "Bull said he was having chest pains and was taken to the infirmary. He somehow knocked out the EMT on duty and escaped."

The details of that escape were definitely sketchy, but it wouldn't stay that way. Jesse would want to hear exactly what'd happened because he needed to know if Bull had had any help getting out. The man had plenty of friends and even a sibling who might do his bidding to give him a second shot at getting revenge.

"Your family knows?" Hanna asked.

Jesse nodded again, and he tipped his head, motioning for her to follow him out of the nursery. Evan was asleep, but he didn't want the possibility of the baby picking up on anything he was saying. Of course, Evan was too young to understand the words or the danger. However, he might pick up on the vibes. Or Hanna's fear. Because Jesse knew that her fear was there and already skyrocketing.

"My family knows," Jesse assured her once they were out in the hall.

On the five-minute drive from the Silver Creek Sheriff's Office to Hanna's place on the edge of town, he'd called Boone Ryland, the man who'd adopted and raised him and his siblings after their widowed mother, Melissa, had married him when Jesse was ten. That adoption had given Jesse six more brothers and numerous cousins, many of whom carried a badge or were retired law enforcement. By now, Boone had no doubt informed the entire family, and they all had already started taking security measures.

Just as Jesse was about to do.

"Bull's never made a threat to come after you," Jesse reminded Hanna. "You were what he'd consider accidental collateral damage."

Bad collateral damage and a case of wrong place, wrong time.

Hanna had had the misfortune of coming to Jesse's house on the grounds of the Ryland family's Silver Creek Ranch to drop off photos of the latest ultrasound and some medical consent forms she had wanted him to sign. She'd been at the massive wrought-iron security gates that fronted the property at the exact moment Bull and his cohort, Arnie Ross, had arrived to confront Boone before they could be arrested.

To confront Jesse, too.

Boone had been the one to get the tip about Arnie and Bull being part of a dangerous gun-running militia. A tip that'd come from an old friend who was now a retired San Antonio cop. Boone had passed the info along to Jesse and the other lawmen in the Silver Creek Sheriff's Office, and that, in turn, had spurred a full-scale investigation.

Since there'd been a security camera mounted on the gate, Jesse had caught glimpses of how everything had gone to hell in a handbasket the night Bull and Arnie had come for that confrontation. The men had both exited Arnie's truck and had words with Hanna, who had arrived just seconds earlier. Exactly what words, Jesse didn't know since there'd been no audio on the camera and Hanna couldn't remember because of the brain trauma.

Whatever had been said had obviously caused Arnie to snap. Maybe because he'd been high. Maybe because he just had a very short fuse. Along with being a serious drug user and a member of that notorious militia group, Arnie had also been on the verge of being arrested, and he'd been the one to drag Hanna out of her car.

Something that Bull damn sure hadn't stopped.

Nor had Bull stopped Arnie from shooting out the camera. But that hadn't happened before Jesse had seen Hanna, and it was an image that was forever branded in his mind.

Jesse had witnessed the stark fear on Hanna's face while she'd tried to keep her hand protectively over her pregnant belly. Arnie had then started running with her. So had Bull. They'd disappeared into a cluster of thick oaks about fifteen yards from the gate.

That's where Jesse had found them.

After the frantic race to get to Hanna. After he'd heard the two shots. After everything inside had pinnacled in a red haze of fury and sickening dread.

Jesse had found Hanna on the ground, shot and bleeding.

Arnie had been shot and bleeding, too, and he was no longer the one holding the gun. Bull was. Arnie had used his dying breath to say that Bull had shot both of them when Hanna had struggled to get away. The .38 jacketed bullet had hit her in the frontal lobe of her brain.

Immediate surgery had saved Evan's and Hanna's lives. But not her memories. There were times when Jesse thought that was more of a blessing than a curse.

Jesse expected her to blow off his reminder that Bull hadn't intentionally targeted her, to give in to the fear that had to be crawling its way through her right now. But she didn't. Standing across from him, Hanna released a long, slow sigh and leaned back against the wall, but she also seemed to be steadying herself. Her hands certainly weren't shaking any longer.

"But Bull has threatened you," she pointed out, putting some of that steel in her voice. "And your father."

Yeah, he had indeed. Bad blood sometimes turned ugly, and that's what had happened with Bull and Boone. Even before Boone had gotten the tip about Bull being in the militia, there had been a land dispute that had escalated into a lawsuit and more than a year of ill will.

Of course, Bull had denied being in the militia. The man had also claimed that shooting Hanna and Arnie had been purely an accident, that the gun had gone off when he'd tried to wrestle it from his buddy, Arnie, and that he'd never intended Hanna and the baby any real harm. The last part might have been true.

Back then anyway.

But with six months of prison under his belt, Bull might be willing to act on that bad blood by going after anyone and everyone in the Ryland clan. If so, that gave the man a hell of a lot of targets. Dozens, what with Boone's kids, grandkids, nieces and nephews. Friends, too, who might be on Bull's hit list. That meant anyone in Silver Creek could become another victim of Bull's so-called collateral damage.

"Have you had your security system on for the past couple of hours?" Jesse asked her just to verify.

"Yes, and I haven't gone outside." She paused. "It was a tough day because I couldn't stop thinking about tomorrow, when Bull's trial starts. Or rather, when he *was* due back in court."

Jesse certainly hadn't forgotten that, and he'd figured it would be hard on Hanna.

Bull had been put in jail, yes, but there was always the possibility that a jury would buy his insistence that it was an accidental shooting. Added to that, the trial meant going over all the details of what'd happened to her. Details she couldn't remember. Couldn't confirm. And that might sway a jury, too, in the wrong direction.

So, why had Bull escaped when there'd been the looming possibility that he could walk out of that courtroom as a free man? Well, free of the charges against Hanna and Arnie anyway. Eventually, he would have to stand trial for his participation in the militia.

"I looked out the window a couple of times but didn't see anyone or anything," Hanna added a moment later. "You think he'll come here?"

No way could he try to lie to her or give her false hope. "I think that's a strong possibility," Jesse answered.

Hanna nodded, and she clamped her teeth over her trembling bottom lip. He would have added a whole lot more if his phone hadn't buzzed with an incoming call. When Jesse saw the name on the screen, he knew he had to answer it right away.

"It's Grayson," he relayed to Hanna.

Sheriff Grayson Ryland, who was Jesse's adopted brother and the oldest of the Ryland siblings. He was also the law in Silver Creek, for the next couple of months anyway until his well-earned retirement.

"Just making sure you're with Hanna and that everything's secured," Grayson said the moment Jesse answered.

"I am and it is," Jesse verified and, after giving it a couple seconds of thought, he put the call on speaker. It was possible Hanna would hear something in this conversation that would upset her even more than she already was, but Jesse didn't want to keep anything from her. "I'm with Hanna now, and she's listening. Has anyone reported seeing Bull?" He'd tacked the question on.

"Not yet, but they found the EMT's truck that Bull used to escape. It was abandoned on a side road about ten miles from the prison. An *isolated* side road," Grayson emphasized.

"Has anyone reported a stolen vehicle in the area?" Jesse immediately asked. Because a remote area meant Bull had needed some way to get out of there, and Jesse doubted the man planned to walk to whatever destination he had in mind, especially since he would have likely still been wearing an orange prison jumpsuit.

"No reported stolen vehicles," Grayson attested. "And Bull didn't have the EMT's phone."

Jesse cursed under his breath because it meant this escape had likely been set up so that Bull could flee the prison and meet up with someone at that specific location. Someone who'd aided and abetted the escape. Someone who at this very moment could be helping Bull get to Silver Creek to carry out whatever plan he had in mind.

"You need me to start the process to access Bull's visitors' log at the prison and question all of his cronies from the militia?" Jesse asked.

"All of that is already in the works. Most of the militia members went under and disappeared after his arrest, but I'm sure we can find a couple of them. I'll also pay a visit to his sister."

Good. Because even though Bull's sister, Marlene, didn't have a criminal record and hadn't showed any support for him after his arrest, it didn't mean Bull hadn't talked her into helping him. And even if she'd turn down any request for help, she might still know where he was.

"There are no indications that the EMT was involved in the escape," Grayson went on. "He has a clean record, and there are no suspicious funds in his bank account. Bull punched him, and when he hit the floor, it knocked him out. He's got a concussion."

Jesse heard the slight groan that Hanna tried to silence by pressing her fingers to her mouth. She'd seen Bull at the hearing where he'd pleaded not guilty to murder and attempted murder, and she knew the guy was plenty big and strong. His nickname definitely suited him.

"Dad and your mom are at my house," Grayson continued a moment later. "Everyone here is on alert."

Good. His folks could likely protect themselves, but it was better for them to be with family right now. Jesse intended to be on alert, as well, and it'd stay that way until Bull was back where he belonged.

"What's your status there?" Grayson asked.

"No sign of Bull, and Hanna's had her security system on all day. I'm about to work things out with her," Jesse assured him and added a "Keep me posted" before Grayson and he ended the call.

Slipping his phone back into his pocket, Jesse met Hanna's gaze head-on. "I either need to stay the night here with you or move Evan and you to my place on the ranch."

It wasn't an ordinary ranch either. The Rylands' sprawling Silver Creek Ranch had hundreds of acres, more than a dozen houses, and enough lawmen to staff an entire small-town police force.

But it was also the place where Hanna had been shot.

Even though Hanna didn't have memories of that, she'd unfortunately seen the photos of the aftermath. Partially as a result of the psychologist trying to help her regain her memories. Other times as a result of glimpses of them when she'd visited the sheriff's office to give statements or for pretrial briefings.

"I don't think I can be at the ranch," she muttered. "I haven't had a panic attack in weeks, but I think just being there might trigger one."

Yeah, he'd figured that. "Being here could trigger one, too."

She nodded so fast that he understood she'd already come to that particular conclusion. "I have to make sure Evan stays safe, and that means me being as mentally sharp as I can manage. It won't help him if I lose it and give in to the panic."

His own nod was equally fast. "If I stay here, I can have some of the ranch hands come over and patrol the grounds." Something he was certain was already going on at the ranch.

This was obviously a rock and a hard place for Hanna. She didn't want him to be this big of a part of her life. Maybe because he was a blank spot when it came to her memories, but he suspected it went deeper than that. After all, she knew from the police reports of her attack that he'd been there that fateful night.

And that he hadn't been able to stop Bull from shooting her.

There was a bottom line to this, and it was a bad one. She wouldn't have been in Bull's path that night at all if it hadn't been for him. Because he hadn't been able to stop Bull when he'd had the chance. Even though for Hanna it was something she couldn't remember, her mother no doubt reminded her of it often.

"All right," Hanna finally said, pushing herself away from the wall. "Call for the ranch hands to come over. You can stay in the guest room. If Bull isn't back in custody by morning, I'll come up with a long-range plan."

That tightened his jaw because she was no doubt talking about private security. Bodyguards, maybe extra monitoring equipment. And while he was on the same page with her about keeping Evan safe, Jesse intended to stay with his son until the danger had passed.

However, that was an argument he'd save for when it came up.

For now, he fired off the text to the head ranch hand, asking for two armed men to keep watch. When he'd finished and gotten the "will do" response, he went looking for Hanna.

He walked past her bedroom, where Jesse got a jolt

of memories. Ones not associated with being pissed off about her *long range* plan. Nope, these particular memories were sizzling hot and reminders that the one and only time he'd ever had sex with Hanna, it'd been in that bedroom.

There were only two other rooms off this particular hall. A bathroom and her guest room, which she was obviously doubling as an art studio. Hanna was in there, and she sighed when she looked at the bed that she apparently used for preparing her paintings for shipping. There were five of them and another on the easel. A watercolor of the Texas Hill Country, her specialty. And she was darn good at it, too. Enough for her to earn a comfortable living even though she no longer taught art classes.

"I've been using this room instead of the studio," Hanna explained. "So I can be close to Evan when I'm painting. The studio's small, and I didn't want to expose him to the smells from the paint and the brush cleaners. Plus, there's no security system out there."

That made sense. "Don't worry about moving the paintings," Jesse told her. "I won't be getting much sleep tonight. If I get too tired, I'll just crash on the couch."

She made a sound of agreement, maybe because she figured she wouldn't be getting much sleep, either, and she took a quilt and pillow from the closet. She handed them to him and pulled out a second quilt.

"For me," she said. "I'll stay in the nursery with Evan."

No way would Jesse try to talk her out of that. It

was probably overkill but, at the moment, no precaution seemed too much for them to take. In fact, he just might end up in the hall outside the nursery door. That way, they could both make sure Bull didn't get close to the baby.

Hanna opened her mouth again, maybe to voice the worries that he knew had to be eating away at her, but she must have changed her mind about that because she just shook her head.

"Let me know if you need anything," Hanna added, already turning toward the nursery.

Jesse watched her go in and was about to head to the living room when his phone buzzed again. It was a soft sound, but Hanna must have heard it because she hurried back to him.

"It's Grayson," he told her and, as he'd done before, Jesse put the call on speaker.

"Make sure everything's secure," Grayson immediately said. "Bull's just been sighted in Silver Creek."

Chapter Two

Breathe, Hanna reminded herself. She tried a trick that her doctor had recommended to help her with the panic attacks. She brought up the image of her son in her mind.

The image of Evan smiling and babbling.

As usual, it slowed her racing heart, but she knew she would no doubt need a lot more steeling up to listen to the rest of what Grayson had to say.

"Where was Bull spotted?" Jesse asked the sheriff while he walked to the front window to look out.

Hanna went with him, and she grabbed the baby monitor from the foyer table so she could keep an eye on Evan while she also looked to see if a killer was nearby. Yes, she would definitely need more steeling up.

"Out on Miller Road," Grayson answered. "Sheri Cartwright was driving home from work and said she saw Bull behind the wheel of a black truck. He was going in the opposite direction from her."

Hanna was familiar with the road since it was only about a mile from her house. Much too close. She was familiar with the name Sheri Cartwright, too, and was told that they'd been friends in high school.

"It's dark," Jesse pointed out. "You think Sheri could be mistaken about it being Bull?"

"No, I think she saw him. It hasn't hit the media yet about Bull's escape, so Sheri wasn't actually looking for the man. She said she passed him and when she caught a quick glimpse of his face, she did a sort of mental double take at seeing him out and about. She decided to call the sheriff's office."

Good thing that she had made that call because at least now they had a heads-up about Bull being so close. Of course, Hanna knew a heads-up wouldn't stop the man from trying to get onto her property and into the house.

So he could try to kill her.

But Bull had to know that Jesse would be there with her, that he would do whatever it took to protect Evan and her. Bull, though, might be in the "whatever it takes" mode as well. He could be willing to take all kinds of risks to get to Jesse and her.

"I don't suppose Sheri got a look at the license plate of the truck Bull was driving?" Jesse pressed.

"No, and she didn't have much of a description for the vehicle itself either. Older model, black or dark blue. That's it. We'll get out the word, ask if anyone's missing a truck like that or if one was recently sold in the area. We might get lucky."

Grayson didn't sound especially hopeful. Neither was Hanna. She'd done a lot of reading about Bull in the past couple of months and knew he was a smart man. He was not only former military, but he'd also run a successful real estate business before moving to Silver Creek three years earlier. If he'd arranged this escape, then he would likely have also arranged to trade out vehicles to throw the cops off his trail.

She had also done some reading about the militia group that Bull had been part of. The Brotherhood. According to the reports Hanna found, there had been at least a hundred members, and they'd been involved in all sorts of illegal activity including weapons, drugs and perhaps even human trafficking.

What was missing from those reports was why Bull had gotten involved with a group like that in the first place. He'd gone to school with Arnie Ross, the man who'd taken Hanna from her car, so maybe that was the link. Or maybe Bull had just gotten greedy and wanted a piece of the lucrative illegal deals being made. Added to that, his real estate business would have been a good place to launder any money from those ill-gotten gains.

"I sent two of the reserve deputies out to Miller Road," Grayson continued. "And I'll get out the word to make sure anyone who sees Bull reports it."

"It wasn't smart, though, for Bull to come to Silver Creek," she muttered.

Until she heard the words, Hanna hadn't even known she was going to say them, but it was the truth. He might not have lived in Silver Creek that long, but he would still be very recognizable since his name had been plastered all over the news.

"No, not smart," Jesse and Grayson agreed in unison.

"But this means he's taking unnecessary risks,"

Jesse continued a moment later. "And it'll make it easier for us to catch him."

True. But Hanna knew Bull might shoot someone else before the cops were able to stop him.

"Bull's sister lives close to Miller Road," Jesse pointed out.

"Yeah. I'm going over to check on her now," Grayson explained. "You'll be moving Hanna and Evan to the ranch?"

A muscle flickered in Jesse's jaw. "Not tonight."

Grayson's jaw had probably gone a little tight, too, and Hanna hoped she wasn't making a huge mistake by wanting to stay put. Still, if she was truly Bull's target, he would come after her no matter where she was. Ditto for Boone. And since he probably wanted Boone more than he did her, then that was even more reason to steer clear of the Ryland ranch.

That could also put her even closer to Jesse.

Of course, he was close now and would be staying the night. Hanna wanted that, for Evan's safety, but being around Jesse was never easy. Yes, the heat was there between them but, as her mother so often reminded her, Jesse and his family were the reason she'd been shot, the reason she had come so close to losing her precious baby before he'd even been born.

The logical part of her knew the Rylands hadn't intended for her to be shot, but it was hard for her to trust them. To trust anyone. Without the memories, there were just too many blank spots, which meant there were too many doubts. Plus, she'd proved that her instincts weren't that stellar since she had been told she was the one who'd decided to go to the ranch that night Bull had shot her.

"I'll let you know what I find out from Marlene," Grayson finally said before he ended the call.

Jesse slipped his phone back in his pocket and met her gaze for a couple of seconds before he turned his attention back to keeping watch out the window.

She didn't need memories to know what was going through his head. He loved Evan. She had no doubts about that. And he wanted to keep their son safe. But he probably felt safety was better met at the ranch.

Where her life as she'd known it had ended.

For all intents and purposes, her life had begun six months ago, and her first memories had been waking up in the hospital. She had been in pain, *so much pain*, and terrified. She hadn't even known she'd had a child, one delivered by an emergency C-section, until several hours after she'd awakened.

Little by little, Jesse, her mother and the medical staff had filled her in, but other than Evan, it hadn't felt real. More like hearing a story about someone else's life. It was still like that.

Except for the heat between Jesse and her.

No way could she deny that they had once been attracted enough to one another to have sex. No. Because the attraction was still there. Of course, she figured most women would be attracted to Jesse.

He wasn't a Ryland by blood, but she'd seen others in that family and knew the men were undeniably hot. Jesse was no exception with his dark hair and sizzling brown eyes. This cowboy cop had it all.

The toned and tanned body. The thick, rumpled hair that looked as if he'd just gotten out of bed. And the strong jaw, sporting just enough stubble to add even more character to that face.

As if it needed that.

Her first memory of Jesse was seeing him in the doorway of her hospital room shortly after she'd been moved out of recovery from her C-section. He'd been wearing jeans that day, too, and a blue shirt. It'd had blood on it.

Her blood, she later learned.

Hanna remembered the penetrating look in his eyes that had robbed her of her breath. She hadn't understood that intensity at the time. Hadn't known the guilt he'd no doubt been feeling. Hadn't known he was the father of a son she'd yet to see or hold. But even with her mind whirling and nothing making sense, she had understood that this man was somehow connected to her. And always would be.

She yanked herself out of her untimely trip down memory lane and snapped her eyes to the window when she heard the sound of an approaching engine. Her heart went into overdrive, causing the blood to rush to her head. She fought the instinct to run to the nursery and watched as the silver muscle truck pulled to a stop in front of her house. The logo on the side of the driver's door let her know these were the hands from the Silver Creek Ranch.

Two cowboys got out, both armed with rifles, and one greeted Jesse with a nod and then motioned toward the east side of her property, where he headed. The other one went to the west.

"They're good men," Jesse said, maybe because he'd glanced back at her and had seen the apprehension in her eyes.

The ranch hands were a necessary safeguard. She wanted them there. But they were still strangers to her, and that always brought on a fresh wave of alarm.

"Breathe," Jesse murmured to her.

Since he'd witnessed firsthand one of her panic attacks, he no doubt knew the signs and had recognized how things could quickly spin out of control for her. That's why she took his advice and tried to level her breathing while also going through one of her "anchoring" steps.

Hanna set down her phone and the baby monitor so she could apply pressure to the skin between her thumb and index finger on her left hand. She kept pressing, kept locking on to the image of a smiling Evan, until she had the anxiety better under control, until the sound of her throbbing heartbeat got quieter and slower in her ears.

Jesse continued to volley his attention between her and the front window, and he watched until she had steadied herself enough to pick up the monitor and her phone again.

"I'm okay," she assured him, which, of course, was a lie.

She was far from okay, but she couldn't let something like panic interfere with her helping Jesse. That meant she, too, needed to be keeping watch for Bull.

That's why she went to the side window. It was only a few feet from where Jesse was standing, but it would give her a different view from his. A view that might allow her to spot Bull before he got into a position where he could do some more harm.

Her phone dinged with a call, the sound startling her, and she silently cursed when she saw her mother's name on the screen. Hanna knew she should have already contacted her mom and told her the same lie about being okay.

Drawing in another deep breath, Hanna answered while she continued to keep watch outside. Unlike Jesse, Hanna didn't put this call on speaker. No need for him to hear what was no doubt about to be said. Over the past six months, Hanna had learned just how much venom her mother had for Jesse and the rest of the Rylands.

"I had to learn about that horrible man's escape from one of the nurses who's got family in Silver Creek," her mother immediately greeted. "I'm coming over there right now to stay with Evan and you. I had my assistant bring me a car a couple of weeks ago, and I can be there in under an hour."

"No, please don't come." Hanna couldn't say that fast enough.

For one thing, her mother, Isabel, was recovering from a recent stroke and was still convalescing in an upscale nursing home in San Antonio. There was no way she should be behind the wheel of a car. Of course, her assistant shouldn't have brought her a vehicle, either, but that was a beef for Hanna to tackle some other time.

"But you shouldn't be alone," her mother protested.

"I'm not alone. Jesse's here and so are two armed ranch hands."

Hanna had already anticipated her mother's disapproving silence, so it didn't come as a surprise. Neither did the continued protest that immediately followed.

"I'll make some calls," Isabel insisted, going into the full "protective mom" mode. "I'll get some bodyguards out there ASAP. I can also call a friend in the Texas Rangers to take over the hunt for the man who nearly killed you."

"Please don't do any of that." Hanna kept her tone respectful, but it wasn't always easy to do that with her mom. Especially when Isabel rarely bothered to keep her own tone in check. "Jesse's staying the night, and Grayson already has someone out looking for Bull. It's possible the sheriff's office will soon have him back in custody."

"The Rylands." Isabel spat the name out like a profanity. "You should't be putting your life and Evan's in their hands."

Again, this was no surprise because it was an opinion that Isabel often voiced. Hanna might have reservations about ever getting intimately involved with Jesse again, but she didn't doubt his commitment to Evan. Isabel probably didn't doubt it, either, not really, but since the woman had bad blood with the Rylands, she would likely never want to believe anything but the worst about any of them.

Hanna had only gotten Isabel's side of the story, but the bad blood had started when Hanna had been a toddler, and Grayson, who'd been a deputy at the time, had arrested Hanna's father for assaulting a young woman. Isabel had insisted the assault hadn't happened and had equally insisted that her husband hadn't been having an affair with the battered woman. Isabel had fought the charges even though they'd led to her husband's conviction and subsequent parole.

Since Hanna's father had died of a heart attack shortly thereafter, she wasn't sure she would ever know the full truth. She certainly didn't expect to ever get it from Isabel, but from everything she'd heard, her father had indeed been cheating, and he had a vicious temper that could have spurred the attack.

"Did you hear me?" Isabel snapped. "You can't trust the Rylands. You can't trust them with your life or Evan's."

"It'll be fine," Hanna said, knowing that wouldn't come close to soothing her mom. "I'll call you in the morning with an update." Hanna ended the call. No need to drag out what would only escalate into an argument.

Even though Hanna only had six months of memories when it came to her mother, she'd learned that Isabel could be stubborn and demanding. She wasn't in the mood to deal with that tonight. But she also didn't want the woman in harm's way, and that's exactly where she could be if she tried to drive to Silver Creek.

Hanna quickly texted her mother's doctor, Michael

Warner, and told him about the possibility that Isabel might try to leave the facility. Dr. Warner would make sure that she stayed put. Hanna also asked him to check that everything was secure at the facility and gave him a brief explanation about Bull's escape from prison. The doctor would no doubt see to that, too, since it could put some of the other residents in danger if by some long shot Bull showed up there.

"Isabel didn't approve of me being here at your place," Jesse commented when Hanna finally set her phone aside. It wasn't a question.

"She didn't," Hanna verified. She sighed. "It's funny. Most people have given me plenty of space since I lost my memory. But not her. Part of me understands that, because I'm a mother, too. Still..." She trailed off, leaving it at that.

Best not to get into the frustrations. Or the fact that she wished Isabel would get on board with giving her that space.

"Your mother wants Evan and you safe," Jesse said, using that soothing drawl that was now so familiar. It spun through her like warm honey.

Hanna didn't doubt that about her mother's intentions, but Isabel could be overwhelming, and that was the main reason Hanna had resisted her mother's pressure to move into the family estate with her. The estate wasn't far, just on the other side of Silver Creek, but she didn't want to be under Isabel's thumb 24/7, especially since being there would make it next to impossible for Jesse to come and visit his son.

"It isn't always easy," Hanna murmured when she

realized Jesse was giving her that look. Not the heated one that he sometimes wasn't able to shut down fast enough. This was essentially a raised eyebrow, without the actual gesture, that was asking her to explain her *still* comment about her mother.

He nodded in that same slow way as his drawl and rephrased. "I'd imagine it's rarely uncomplicated for you these days. I'm sorry about that." Jesse shook his head and said something under his breath she didn't catch. "Sorry you're having to go through this on top of everything else you've had to deal with."

She didn't have to remember him well to know it was guilt she was hearing in his voice. Hanna had heard it plenty of times before. Had seen it, too, and it was just as strong as her mother's insistence that the Rylands were to blame for what had happened to her.

Hanna shifted her attention to the baby monitor when she saw Evan squirm a little. He shouldn't be anywhere close to waking up yet, but there were still times when he didn't sleep through the night. She had her attention on the baby when Jesse's phone beeped again.

"It's Grayson," Jesse relayed.

That got her attention, and it only took a few seconds before Grayson's voice poured through the room. "Marlene's not at her house. There are signs of a struggle. And blood," he added.

Hanna's heart dropped to her knees. Oh, mercy. This had to be Bull's doing. The man had gone after someone else.

"There's an old black truck parked at the back of her house," Grayson went on. "It might be the one

Bull was driving when Sheri saw him. Also, Marlene's car isn't in the garage."

So that probably meant Bull had taken his sister in her own vehicle. Had maybe even killed her. Or he could be planning on using her as a hostage if he got cornered by the cops.

"You need me to call and put out an APB on Marlene?" Jesse asked.

"No, I'll take care of it. I just wanted you to know in case you saw a silver Lexus near Hanna's place." Grayson rattled off the license plate of what was no doubt Marlene's vehicle. "Marlene also has a permit for a Beretta. It's my guess I won't find it here at her house."

Hanna was betting the same thing, which meant Bull was now armed. Perhaps had money, too, since Marlene would have almost certainly had some cash at her place.

"Keep watch and stay safe," Grayson said.

Even though the sheriff ended the call, Jesse stared at his phone still gripped in his hand. Shaking his head as if trying to clear his thoughts, he had just turned back to the window when he got another incoming call.

Hanna hadn't relaxed or let down her guard one bit, but she experienced another rush of adrenaline because she thought it was Grayson with yet more horrible news.

"It's Dispatch," Jesse muttered, putting the call on speakerphone.

She pulled in her breath. Held it. And waited.

She didn't have to wait long before she heard the

familiar voice. Not Grayson or one of the other Silver Creek lawmen.

"It's me," the caller said.

Bull.

This time it was much more than an adrenaline crash. This was like an avalanche of emotions, yanking her right back to the pain of her injury. Right back to the nightmare she knew this man had put her through.

"Where are you?" Jesse growled, sounding exactly like the tough lawman that he was.

Bull obviously ignored the demand.

"We have to talk. There's a whole lot going on you don't know about, and it could get us all killed."

Chapter Three

Jesse heard every word that Bull had just said, but he didn't respond. Didn't believe him either.

Not for one second.

But the reason Jesse didn't reply was that he fired off a text to the dispatcher and asked for an immediate trace on the call just in case that hadn't already been set into motion. Bull was likely using a burner since he hadn't taken the EMTs phone, but if Bull was using a stolen phone, then a trace was still possible.

Jesse also continued to keep watch out the window because he wouldn't put it past Bull for this phone call to be some kind of ploy, a distraction so he could try to sneak up on them.

Jesse did a quick visual check on Hanna. Thankfully, she didn't look on the verge of a panic attack like the one he'd witnessed shortly after she'd gotten out of the hospital. She was clearly shaken by hearing from the man who'd come way too close to killing her, but she was holding it together. She was also looking out, no doubt scanning the grounds for Bull.

He moved to her, taking hold of her arm as he'd

done earlier in the doorway, and Jesse eased her to the side of the window. Best not to give Bull an easy target in case he was close enough to the house to start shooting.

Stay back, Jesse mouthed to her, and the reminder of the possibility of her being shot had her attention flying back to the baby monitor.

Jesse had already considered the position of his son's crib. Away from the windows and tucked against a wall with the adjoining bath. There were no guarantees that a bullet couldn't make it through there, but there was no place in the house they could move the baby to ensure that didn't happen. However, if they or the ranch hands did spot Bull, Jesse would have Hanna take Evan into the bathtub. For now, though, he didn't want to wake his son unless it became necessary.

"Did you hear me?" Bull snarled. "I said this mess could get us all killed."

Jesse had no doubts about that, but he figured there was no "us" in this scenario. Bull would be the one doing the killing. He was puzzled, though, as to what the heck the man meant by "this mess." However questions about that would have to wait since there was something else at the top of the list of things Jesse needed to know.

"Where are you?" Jesse countered.

"Trying to get some place safe so I won't be gunned down. Just tell your cowboy cop friends that all isn't what it seems and not to shoot first without asking questions. The *right* questions," Bull emphasized.

"And what would the right questions be?" Jesse prodded, not only because he wanted to know where this was leading, but also because he wanted to give the dispatcher time to trace the call.

It was possible Bull was using a burner that couldn't be traced, but he could also be using his sister's cell. If so, they might be able to ping a location. Unfortunately, from the background noise Jesse was picking up, it sounded as if the man was driving. That would make pinpointing his whereabouts a lot harder.

"Questions about what really went on that night Hanna was shot." Bull stopped, cursed. "None of this should have happened."

Yeah, Jesse could agree with that, too. "If you hadn't tried to evade arrest, no one would have been hurt or killed," Jesse pointed out. He didn't wait for Bull to react to that. Instead, Jesse went with some important questions. "Where's your sister? Is she still alive?"

"My sister?" Bull seemed genuinely surprised by the question. *Seemed.* "What about Marlene? Did something happen to her?"

"You tell me," Jesse responded, and he kept it at that.

"What the hell is wrong with my sister?" Bull demanded.

Jesse had plenty of bad feelings about this little chat, but he had to wonder if Bull had already killed Marlene and was trying to make it sound as if he'd had no part in that.

"Turn yourself in, and you'll find out what happened to Marlene," Jesse countered.

He figured that would cause Bull to keep up the innocent act, but the man cursed and Jesse heard the sound of brakes squealing. Not nearby, but from Bull's end of the phone connection.

What the heck was Bull doing? Was it possible he was changing directions so he could go to Marlene? If that was the case, Jesse sent another quick text to Grayson to alert him of that possibility.

"You need to ask yourself about what really took place that night Hanna was shot." Bull threw it out there. "Then you'll find out the truth."

With that, the man ended the call, leaving Jesse with a whole lot of questions. That bad feeling he was already having went up a couple more notches.

"What did he mean?" Hanna immediately asked. "Are you keeping something from me about the shooting?"

"No." Jesse couldn't answer fast enough. "I haven't kept anything from you." It was important for her to hear that, to believe it, because he didn't need to have her distrusting him right now. Besides, it was the truth. "As for what Bull meant, I don't know. Could be he's just trying to muddy the waters."

If so, it had created some mud, all right, and Jesse had to at least consider the possibility that Bull hadn't had a part in Marlene's disappearance. Even though it would be one hell of a coincidence, there was a chance that what'd happened to the woman had had nothing to do with her brother. Marlene was a wealthy woman who lived alone; someone else could have broken in and kidnapped her. Still, Jesse's money was on Bull for this.

"'You need to ask yourself about what really took place that night Hanna was shot,'" she said, repeating Bull's words. "Are there any doubts or questions about what Bull did that night?"

Five minutes ago, Jesse would have said no, but he forced himself to go over it again. Not that it was ever too far from his thoughts. But it was possible to miss something when a case or investigation was personal. This one had been as personal as it could get.

"One of the ranch hands heard a commotion at the gate," he said, spelling it out for her. He hoped that by saying it aloud again, he'd notice any gray areas that might answer her concerns, and his, about what Bull had just told them. "It was already dark, but he used his phone app to look at the security camera. He saw the two vehicles—your car and Arnie's truck. There was no audio, but since the ranch hand thought there was some kind of argument going on, he called me and Noah."

No need for Jesse to explain that Noah was another cop and someone who'd been raised on the ranch. Or that the reason the hand had contacted both of them was that he'd known they were home and could make a quick response.

"When Noah and I approached the gate, Arnie had already pulled you out of your car," Jesse went on. "We think he did that to use you as a human shield so we couldn't arrest him."

"He knew for a fact you were going to arrest him?" Hanna asked.

This was yet something else Jesse had already answered, but he tried to see it with fresh eyes. "Bull and he both knew arrests were imminent. Grayson had them scheduled for questioning the following morning, and he'd advised them to bring their lawyers." Jesse paused. Because he had to do that. He needed a moment to try to rein in what guilt he could. "I should have expected they'd panic and would try to do something stupid."

"Is that because they'd done something stupid before?" she quickly challenged. "I mean, had they ever come to the ranch to confront Boone or you?"

"No," Jesse had to admit. But it was still something he should have anticipated. "Since Arnie and Bull knew they would be arrested, that obviously escalated their need to go through with the confrontation."

Hanna stayed quiet a moment. "But instead of confronting Boone and you, they tried to take me. Maybe because something I said provoked one of them?"

His gaze fired to hers. "There's nothing you could have said that should have provoked them to do what they did." Jesse wanted to make that crystal clear. She'd been the victim in this. Evan and her. He didn't want her shouldering any of the blame that should be her attackers'.

And his.

"Bull's been vague about what led up to the escalation," Jesse continued. "We do know from the security camera footage that Arnie first tried to get you into his truck, but he dropped his keys and apparently didn't see them on the ground. They didn't get in your car because Arnie's truck was behind it, blocking it. That's when Bull and Arnie seemed to have panicked and fled into the trees with you."

Jesse stopped, took in another much-needed deep breath. None of this was new to Hanna. She'd heard and read about it heaven knew how many times. But she also knew these next few minutes were blind spots for all of them.

Except Bull, that is.

"It's possible Bull just told us what he did to try to make up something to put himself in a better light," Jesse reminded her. *You need to ask yourself about what really took place that night Hanna was shot.* "He's desperate, and he probably wants us to believe he wasn't responsible for what happened to you."

He would have added to that, trying to soothe her while still spelling out the reality of the situation, but Jesse heard something that put him on full alert.

"I see somebody in the backyard," Miguel Navarro shouted. He was one of the ranch hands patrolling the grounds.

Jesse didn't waste a second. "Go to the nursery," he told Hanna. "Take Evan into the bathroom. Lock the door and get in the tub with him."

She didn't waste time arguing. Hanna started running toward the hall, but did look over her shoulder at Jesse. "Be careful," she uttered.

He would be, because he couldn't risk doing something stupid, like going outside to confront the wanted man. It could end up causing Hanna and Evan harm. If Bull shot him, that'd be one less barrier against Bull getting into the house.

Since Grayson already had his hands full, Jesse sent a text to the dispatcher and requested immediate backup. This could turn out to be nothing, but considering everything else going on, Jesse figured it was the real deal. Some kind of threat or attack from Bull.

He hurried to the kitchen, where he'd be able to see the backyard, and turned off the lights so he wouldn't be an easy target for Bull or anyone else who might wish to hurt them. Peering out into the darkness, he spotted Miguel, who'd taken cover on the side of a gardening shed. No sign of the other hand, Rex Corbin, but Jesse suspected he was moving in as well.

Jesse resisted the urge to text Miguel to find out exactly what he'd seen and where. The ranch hand didn't need that kind of a distraction and, like the light in the kitchen, it might allow Bull to pinpoint the man's location. Instead, Jesse tried to create his own distraction after he calculated that Hanna would have had time to get Evan into the tub. He also calculated the angle of any shots Bull might take. That particular bathroom wasn't anywhere near the kitchen.

"Bull?" Jesse called out, shouting loud enough so his voice would carry into the backyard. "This is a good way to get yourself killed. Put down any weapons you have and surrender."

No response. Not that Jesse had expected to get one, but he kept watching, trying to pick through the night and see the man. He didn't see Bull, but he heard something else. A hissing sound, followed by a small pop. The kind of noise a firecracker would make.

"He's running away," Miguel yelled, moving out from the shed to take aim. He must not have had a clean shot because he didn't pull the trigger.

Jesse didn't have a shot, either, but that's because he didn't even get a glimpse of the intruder. However, he did get a glimpse of something else.

A fire.

Obviously ignited by some kind of accelerant, the flames shot up the side of Hanna's studio. Hell. The small building might be a good ten yards from the house, but it was still possible for the fire to spread. Or worse. Maybe Bull or whoever was responsible had already set fire to the house as well.

Jesse made a quick call to the dispatcher to send the fire department and alert backup to the danger before he contacted Miguel. He watched as the ranch hand moved back behind cover and took out his phone to answer.

"I've already made the 9-1-1 call," Jesse informed him. "Any sign of fire to the house?"

"None back here. Let me go to the side and I'll have Rex Corbin do the same on his side."

Jesse trusted both men, but he didn't want them hurt. "Don't leave cover if you think this SOB's armed. Could you tell if it was Bull and if he had a gun?"

"Couldn't tell on either count," Miguel answered.

Jesse sighed. "Then stay put and tell Rex to do the

same. Everything is locked down inside, but if that fire starts to spread, let me know. I'll be with Hanna and the baby."

He ended the call and took one last look around the yard, hoping he'd spot Bull or someone else. But he saw nothing. So, Jesse headed to the nursery. Hanna was no doubt terrified for Evan, and he wanted to be close by in case the fire starter had decided not to run after all and instead tried to break into the house.

The nursery door wasn't locked but the one leading into the bathroom was, so Jesse tapped on it. "It's me," he said.

It only took her a couple of seconds to open the door. She wasn't holding Evan but instead had left the sleeping baby wrapped in his blankets in the tub. Good. That would keep him as safe as possible, and it was an added bonus that there were no windows in here. No way for Bull to get in without coming through the door, which Jesse would make sure didn't happen.

He stepped inside the small bathroom and motioned for her to get back in the tub. He would have launched into an explanation as to what was going on, but Hanna spoke first.

"I smell smoke," she whispered.

Jesse nodded. "Someone set fire to your studio."

He got the reaction that he'd expected. Her eyes widened. Her mouth dropped open. But then he saw something else. The anger.

"How dare he put my baby in danger again?"

Jesse was right there with her. Riled to the bone, he would make Bull pay—and pay hard for this.

"The fire department and backup are on the way," Jesse told her. He could hear the wail of sirens in the distance. "And the ranch hands are still keeping watch."

She shook her head, as if trying to process everything and returned to the tub. "Why set a fire?"

Since Jesse had already had a couple of minutes to process things, he thought he might have an answer for that. "It could have been to draw me out."

So Bull could then gun him down. If that was the case, then this was about revenge, pure and simple. Maybe then Bull would have tried to get more revenge on Hanna by firing shots into the house.

But, if so, why hadn't Bull started with the shots?

Bull had no doubt seen the Silver Creek Ranch truck parked out front and would have guessed there were hands on the grounds or in the house. Why take the risk of coming to the studio instead of staying in the tree line and shooting? It was something he intended to ask Bull once he had him in custody.

Jesse's phone dinged and he relayed the text to Hanna. "Grayson will be here in a couple of minutes." He tipped his head to the front of the house. "From the sound of it, the fire engine just pulled up, so I want you to lock yourself back in here until I let you know it's safe."

She didn't argue with him. Not exactly. Hanna shook her head. "Bull might be waiting to shoot you."

Yeah, he might. Hell, he might try to do the same

to Grayson even though the sheriff hadn't been the lead investigator on Bull's case. That's why Jesse would give Grayson a heads-up reminder even though he was certain he would be taking every precaution.

"Be careful," Hanna said as he went to the door. She got out of the tub, no doubt to lock up behind him, but stopped when his phone buzzed again.

This time it was a call, not a text, and it wasn't from Grayson. Though it was a name he recognized: Ryan Shaw. He was the ATF agent Jesse had touched base with after Bull had been taken into custody; the ATF had wanted copies of any info that Jesse had gathered on the militia. Agent Shaw had likely heard about Bull's escape and wanted an update.

"We haven't found Bull yet," Jesse greeted the moment he answered. "But he's been sighted in Silver Creek."

"Yes," Agent Shaw said, and he followed that with a sigh. "Deputy Ryland, you and I need to talk."

Everything inside Jesse went still. It sounded similar to what Bull had said when he'd called. "I'm listening," Jesse assured him.

"I can't do this over the phone. I need to see you, to talk to you in person."

"Not a good time. Bull or one of his cronies just set fire to a building on Hanna Kendrick's property."

This time the ATF agent didn't sigh. He cursed. "I'm on my way out there. And FYI, whoever set that fire, it wasn't Bull."

"How the hell would you know that?" Jesse snapped.

"Because…" Shaw stopped, cursed again. "Deputy Ryland, Bull isn't behind what happened tonight. But there's trouble. Big trouble. Because somebody wants you dead."

Chapter Four

Hanna took one step into her kitchen. And she stopped cold. Not because of who and what she saw. She'd expected to see Jesse feeding Evan in his high chair. After all, Jesse had volunteered to do that while she'd grabbed a quick shower.

What she hadn't expected was the sudden jolt of memories.

At least, she was pretty sure that's what they were. Actual memories. She had a crystal-clear image of a shirtless Jesse standing in her kitchen with the morning sunlight spearing through the window onto him. Of Jesse with his sleep-tousled hair and dreamy bedroom eyes turning to look at her when she walked in. Of Jesse sipping coffee and smiling at her. The kind of smile a man gave a woman when he had just gotten out of her bed—and wanted to head back for a second round.

She felt the flood of heat, both then and now, and it was way too hot considering her son was babbling and having a messy time with the oatmeal. Her focus should have been on her little boy, on the fact that her house was basically on lockdown, with a deputy standing guard and armed ranch hands patrolling the grounds. She should be worrying about whether or not Bull Freeman would try to come after them again and if Agent Ryan Shaw would soon be cleared to pay them a visit. A visit that could maybe give them answers about Bull and the attacks.

She shouldn't be ogling Jesse and feeling this intense attraction.

"Are you okay?" she heard Jesse ask, and that yanked her back from her thoughts. And the heat.

Hanna nearly lied, nearly told him it was nothing, but even a flash of a memory might be the start of others returning. If so, that was something Jesse needed to know. That way, he could confirm it. Or not. If it was the "or not," then she might have to admit her imagination ran wild and hot whenever she was around him.

"You drank coffee from one of the blue mugs," she said, tipping her head to the open-faced cabinet where there was a row of the cobalt-colored cups. There were only four of them and eight of the sunflower-yellow ones. "That morning after you'd stayed the night," Hanna added after he gave her a puzzled look. "The blinds weren't shut then like they are now."

She watched the realization dawn in his eyes as Jesse slowly stood, Evan's oatmeal spoon still in his hand. He nodded. "I was drinking coffee, and you came into the kitchen after you'd gotten dressed. Like now," he muttered.

For just a moment, he got that smile again. But it

vanished in a blink. Hanna didn't think that was because Evan's cheerful babbling had reminded him
they weren't alone. No. It was probably because he
remembered things hadn't gone well shortly after that.
Hanna wasn't sure how much time had passed before
she'd ended things with Jesse but, according to her
mother's account, it hadn't been long before she'd
"come to her senses."

"Ma, Ma," Evan chattered, which got Hanna moving toward him so she could give him a kiss. She got
a smear of oatmeal on her cheek in the process, but
it was worth it. She didn't have to force or rein in
her happiness, or worry about trust, when she was
around her son.

"I can finish feeding him," she said, sitting in the
chair that Jesse had just vacated.

Jesse didn't complain though he would have likely
wanted to continue since giving his son breakfast
wasn't something he got to do very often. However,
he stayed close, watching not just Evan and her but
also making glances out the narrow side window of
the kitchen door. A reminder that the danger was out
there with Bull still at large.

"Agent Shaw will be here soon," Jesse said while
he poured himself a cup of coffee—and he used one
of the cobalt mugs. "FYI, he's riled that Grayson
wouldn't let him on scene last night. He's still insisting its urgent that he talk to us."

"Not urgent enough though for him to tell you
what it was about over the phone," Hanna concluded.

"Exactly. I suspect the agent wants to cut some

kind of deal with Bull. Though why he'd want us in on that, I don't know. That would be between the ATF and the district attorney." He paused, sipped his coffee. "You want to talk about the memory you just had?"

She managed to smile when she got Evan to eat another spoonful of the oatmeal, but she was definitely giving that question some thought. It was a personal, kick-to-the-gut hot kind of memory, and she doubted that discussing it with Jesse would do anything but fire up more of the heat already there between them.

That, in turn, would stir up her frustration.

Even if her memory fully returned, it didn't mean she'd be giving in to that heat and getting back together with Jesse. After all, there was a reason they weren't together, and until she'd had a chance to go over that reason, and know what was true and what was being filtered through her mother's venom, the hot cowboy cop was off limits. Besides, with the danger caused by Bull's escape, she didn't have the mental energy to deal with the personal stuff.

"No, I don't want to talk about it. Not now anyway," she finally answered. She didn't get a chance to add more because Jesse's phone dinged with a text.

"My folks and Noah are here," Jesse said, reading the message. "You remember them."

She did. Again, no recollection of them prior to her being shot, but Boone Ryland and Jesse's mom, Melissa, had come with him several times to visit Evan. She'd met Jesse's cousin, Noah, while she'd still been in the hospital. Noah was a cop, too, at San

Antonio PD. From all accounts, Jesse and he were as close as brothers.

"They're not here about Bull," Jesse explained. "They're just bringing me a change of clothes and want to see Evan for a couple of minutes."

That was a reminder of how stressful this had to be for the entire Ryland clan. There was probably added stress for Boone since he might be blaming himself for the shooting that had nearly killed Evan and her.

Hanna nodded. "Let them in."

Jesse nodded, too, and headed toward the front door while he typed something on his phone. Probably using the app to disengage the security system. Hanna had given him the log-in info and access code the night before since she'd figured he would be coming and going until they had this situation with Bull under control.

She heard the voices when Jesse opened the door and finished feeding Evan the last of the oatmeal. She'd just wiped the baby's face and had taken him from his high chair when the trio came in. Suddenly, the kitchen was filled with Rylands.

Melissa, Boone and Noah all greeted her with smiles that somehow managed to look both friendly and cautious at the same time. Hanna had no idea if they resented her because she'd ditched Jesse or if they considered that Jesse had dodged a bullet by being entangled with someone who couldn't even remember him. Well, not remember him much anyway.

While Melissa went straight to Evan, Boone kept his distance, and he set the overnight bag he'd brought

in on the counter. Tall and lanky, with hair more silver than black, he had to be in his eighties, but he
looked much younger. Fit. Of course, that probably
had something to do with the active part he still took
in running the family ranch.

Noah was fit, too, and sported those amazing
Ryland genes. She suspected he was the spitting
image of Grandfather Boone in his earlier days.

"Da, Da," Evan babbled, reaching out for Jesse
to take him.

"He's growing fast," Melissa remarked, and she
gave Evan's toes a jiggle that caused him to laugh. She
was a good twenty years younger than Boone and had
once been a Silver Creek deputy before she'd married
him and he'd adopted her three children.

"I'm sorry all of this is happening," Boone murmured, aiming that directly at Hanna.

She tried to come up with the right answer to that,
especially since she couldn't just dismiss Bull's escape as not being the serious threat that it was. Hanna
ended up settling for a nod.

"Uncle Grayson will be here soon with Agent
Shaw," Noah explained. He glanced at Melissa, who
was chattering with Evan, and she picked up the rest
of the explanation.

"I thought I could take Evan to the nursery while
Hanna and you talk to the agent," Melissa told Jesse.
"Noah and Boone have to get back, but I drove sepa-
rately so I can stay as long as you need."

Again, Hanna had to think hard before she responded. She truly didn't want Evan to be part of a

discussion about Bull, but with the danger, she also wasn't sure she wanted him out of her sight. Still, Melissa had been a deputy; she knew how to take precautions to make sure her grandchild was safe.

"Thank you," Hanna finally said.

That caused Melissa to beam. She muttered something about reading some books to Evan before she carried the baby into the adjacent living room where there was a basket filled with books.

"Grayson's been sending me updates," Jesse said, shifting his attention to Noah. "But is there anything new on Marlene?"

Noah shook his head. "Still no signs of her, but we know it was her blood that they found in her house. Not a large amount," he added and, considering he glanced at Hanna when he said that, it was likely meant for her benefit. Maybe to try to reassure her that the woman was still alive.

And perhaps she was. Bull could have plans to try to use her as a bargaining tool, and he wouldn't be able to bargain with a dead woman.

"Grayson has the Texas Rangers looking for Marlene," Noah went on. "SAPD, too. Sooner or later, she'll surface."

Hanna hoped that wasn't wishful thinking. They needed to find Marlene because then they'd almost certainly find Bull. Added to that, Marlene could be hurt and terrified, so finding her was critical.

Her heart rate kicked up when she heard a vehicle come to a stop in front of the house. The sound came just as Jesse received another text.

"It's Mason," Jesse announced. His uncle and a reserve Silver Creek deputy. "Grayson's tied up with an interview, so he had Mason bring over Agent Shaw."

"We should be heading out," Noah explained as they made their way to the door with Jesse following right behind them. Boone and he said their goodbyes, Boone stopping to give both his wife and Evan a kiss before leaving.

Hanna heard murmurs of the brief conversation on the porch and, several seconds later, Mason walked in. Even though he spent most of his time running the family ranch, he was still a police officer, and he made one of those sweeping cop glances around the living room and kitchen.

Mason definitely had the tall, dark and hot Ryland looks, but those features were harder on his face, and even though she'd run into him more than a half dozen times, she'd yet to see him smile. He reminded her of one of those Old West cowboys who was always braced and ready for a gunfight. One that he would win hands down. All the Ryland lawmen looked formidable, but Mason topped the heap when it came to that particular trait.

"Agent Ryan Shaw," Mason said, hitching his thumb to the blond-haired man who stepped in behind him. He was a good six inches shorter than Mason and had a stocky build.

"Evan and I can finish our reading in the nursery," Melissa commented, and she thankfully got the baby out of the room.

Jesse shut the front door, locked it and reengaged the security system.

This wasn't a social visit, but Hanna was still about to offer coffee. However, Agent Shaw spoke before she could say anything.

"It wasn't a good idea to delay this visit," Shaw snarled.

Mason's reaction was subtle. A slight lift of his gunmetal eyes to the ceiling. A barely audible huff.

"The agent thinks we should have broken protocol by bringing him to an active crime scene before we could even verify his credentials," Mason responded. He snarled, too, and it was a lot better than Shaw's. "They've been verified." He glanced back at the agent. "I suggest you stop whining and use your time to inform Deputy Ryland and Miss Kendrick why it was all so hell-fired important that you come here."

That caused the agent's jaw to tighten, and it tightened even more when Mason tapped his watch. Obviously, Jesse's uncle had made it clear to Agent Shaw not to waste their time.

"Like I told you on the phone last night," Shaw said, "we have to talk."

"You said a lot of things last night," Jesse countered. "Paraphrasing here, but you insisted Bull didn't set the fire and there was big trouble. You also mentioned someone wanted me dead, but you refused to tell me who or why."

That didn't ease the clamped muscles in Shaw's face. "Because it was something I needed to tell you in person."

"So you said." Jesse's tone was as iron-hard as Mason's glare. "Well, you're here, so tell me."

Shaw certainly didn't jump right in with an explanation. Instead, he slid a glance at Mason. "I need to divulge this info to as few people as possible."

Mason gave him a flat look. "If you think that'll get me to leave, think again. I'm a cop, and that's my nephew and the mother of my great-nephew. I'm staying put unless Jesse or Hanna want me to go."

"Stay," Jesse insisted, and there was plenty of impatience in his expression when he turned back to Shaw. "Are you here to tell me you're trying to work out a deal with Bull?"

Shaw dragged in a long, slow breath. "No, I'm here to tell you something that stays in this room. Bull is a deep cover ATF agent who infiltrated the militia three years ago in order to find its leader and suppliers."

Hanna shook her head and mentally repeated each word. "An ATF agent tried to murder me?" she snapped.

"No," Agent Shaw quickly answered. "Bull wasn't the one who shot you. Arnie did, and Bull shot and killed him before he could fire a second shot that would have almost certainly left you dead."

Again, she went through the mental repeat, but Hanna could already feel the slam of emotions crashing into her. Emotions that came with one huge question—was all of this true? Since she didn't have any real memories of the shooting, Hanna had had to rely on other people's accounts. She so wished she knew what had actually gone on in those trees because she believed with all her heart that it was now coming back to haunt them.

Or kill them.

"If Bull's really an agent, why'd he end up in jail?" Jesse demanded. Obviously, he was considering the truth of this, too.

Shaw sighed and scrubbed his hand over his face. "Since plenty of the militia members were in that same prison, Bull thought he'd be able to find out the name of the leader."

"So, why would Bull escape if he's in such a great position to get intel?" Jesse demanded.

"Because someone ordered a hit on him. I don't know who," Shaw immediately added. "But from the short phone conversation I've had with Bull, he believed his life was in grave danger. Yours, too. Bull heard talk that somebody was going after you because you haven't given up on investigating the militia."

Jesse cursed. "Hell no, I haven't given up. That militia was responsible for Hanna and my son nearly being killed. I won't give up until every last one of them is behind bars."

Shaw looked him straight in the eyes. "And that's why you're a target."

Oh, mercy. *A target.* So, Jesse was probably right about the fire in her studio being set to draw him out. The same person might use Evan or her to try to get him, too.

Jesse must have heard the soft gasp she made because he automatically ran his hand down the length of her arm. "It's okay," he murmured to her. "Just breathe."

He was soothing her. Or rather, trying to do that. Hanna did as he said and breathed, forcing herself to stay level. Focusing in an effort to rein in the panic. She wouldn't get any answers if she lost the battle with the panic right now.

"Who put the hit on Jesse?" she asked the agent, and she managed to add some steel to her voice.

"I don't know, and I haven't been able to have a face-to-face conversation with Bull."

"Why the hell not?" Jesse protested. "If he's really an agent, why wouldn't he go straight to you or somebody else in the ATF?"

This time Shaw wasn't quite so quick to answer and he glanced away when he spoke. "Bull says he's not sure who to trust. He thinks he'll be gunned down if he comes out in the open. We got a lot of the suppliers for both the guns and the drugs, a lot of the militia members, too. But we still don't know who's running the operation."

"Arnie?" Jesse suggested.

Shaw's headshake was fast and firm. "No. He didn't have the brains for it."

"Certainly, you have suspects then," Jesse said on a huff.

"We do, but so far none of them have panned out. That's why Bull insisted the way to learn the truth was from the other militia members who'd already been arrested. We know the operation has continued, so somebody sure as hell is still running it."

"*Somebody*," Jesse repeated in a cop's tone. He put his hands on his hips and kept his hard stare pinned to the agent. "You're so certain that Bull is clean and has been telling you the truth about the militia?"

Hanna expected Shaw to issue a firm yes in response to Jesse's question. He didn't. Shaw stood there and muttered something she wasn't able to catch.

"No," Shaw finally said. "I can't be positive that he's clean."

Sweet heaven. So it was possible there was a rogue agent out to murder Jesse. Probably her, too, since he couldn't be sure how much she had, or would, remember.

"Here's what I know," Shaw finally went on. "The ATF didn't sanction Bull's escape, and he's refused to come in and talk to me or anyone else in the agency."

"Maybe because he doesn't trust you," Mason quickly pointed out. "Maybe because he knows you're the dirty agent he can't trust."

Shaw didn't jump to deny that, either, but the anger flared in his eyes. "I'm not dirty. But Bull might believe I am. He might think I'm looking for a scapegoat. I'm not," he assured him. "I'm looking for the truth."

"The truth," Jesse grumbled. "And what exactly would that be? Why would Bull suddenly not be trusting his own agency?"

Again, Shaw paused and, judging from the way his jaw muscles were flexing, he was having a battle with himself as to what to say. Or not say.

"I think Bull stopped cooperating with the ATF and me because I got word to him that we have a new suspect," Shaw finally explained. "A suspect he might believe is innocent."

"That scapegoat you mentioned—" Jesse spat out the words "—who is it? Give me a name."

Again, Shaw seemed to have another mental debate before he finally turned his gaze back to Jesse.

"Our prime suspect is Marlene, Bull's sister."

Chapter Five

Marlene.

Jesse had to admit he hadn't seen that particular accusation coming, and he reminded himself that it might be just that.

An accusation.

He didn't know Agent Shaw that well, and the agent might be handing him a load of lies to throw suspicion off himself. Jesse didn't think he had that much in common with Bull but, at the moment, it appeared they shared a mutual distrust of Shaw and the ATF.

"What evidence do you have that Marlene might be the militia leader?" Jesse demanded.

"Evidence that I'm not at liberty to share with you. I'm sorry," Shaw quickly tacked on, "but it involves intel from informants."

"Criminal informants?" Jesse questioned, and even though Shaw didn't confirm or deny that, his steely expression was enough of a confirmation as far as Jesse was concerned.

The info had likely come from one of the jailed

militia members who might or might not be telling the truth. Jesse was going to go with the *might not* in this case because Marlene certainly hadn't been arrested for any crime in Silver Creek. That didn't mean Jesse wouldn't check to make sure she was clean, but for the moment, he would consider her a missing person. One who might be dead or in danger from her brother, a supposed dirty agent.

Yeah, he had plenty of questions.

"Since I'm not sure of Bull's intentions," Shaw continued while he turned to Hanna, "it'd be best for you and your son to be in protective custody. I can arrange for that."

A burst of air left Hanna's mouth. Part laugh, part huff, and with a whole lot of "no thanks" that made Jesse proud of her for standing up to the agent. This danger and fear had to be taking a serious toll on her, but she wasn't just going to run for cover in what could be the wrong place.

"We're already in protective custody," Hanna assured the man. "Jesse's. I think he'll do a much more thorough job of protecting his son than whatever agent you can assign to the task."

"Fine," Shaw grumbled. "Suit yourself. But you might want to remember that Jesse's the target here."

"The possible target," Hanna corrected before Jesse could. "It's also possible that someone planted the info about Jesse being a target to separate him from Evan and me so we'd be easier to take or kill." She tapped her head. "I'm the one who could confirm or dispute Bull's claims."

Shaw's eyes widened. "Your memory's coming back?"

"No." Jesse couldn't say that fast enough. He didn't want Bull or someone else going after Hanna even if it was true.

Or rather, true-ish.

Yeah, she had recalled at least bits and pieces about him being in her kitchen the morning after they'd had sex. Judging from the heat Jesse had also seen in her eyes, she'd maybe recalled the sex, too, but Bull or even Shaw might want to ensure she stayed silent.

"No," Hanna echoed when Shaw just kept that hard stare on her. "My memory isn't coming back. It might never come back, and from what you said, it seems as if your now-rogue agent is responsible for that. You as well."

"Me?" Shaw snarled.

"You," she verified. Her voice was not only stronger, but she also took a step toward Shaw. "Because I don't need to learn all the details of your investigation to know that you should have kept a better leash on Bull. You should have known he was accompanying a desperate, violent militia member to the Silver Creek Ranch and that bystanders, like me and my baby, could have been hurt or killed."

Shaw didn't deny any of that. Couldn't. Because Hanna was right. Even if Bull claimed he had no idea what Arnie was going to do that night, he should have requested some kind of backup from Shaw to deal with Arnie, who'd obviously gotten out of control.

"Mistakes were made," Shaw finally said, clearly

not personally taking any blame. "But remember that Bull saved your life."

Hanna took another step closer to the agent, and even though Jesse could see her hand trembling, she was staying strong. "I don't have a memory of that because Arnie took it away from me. All I have is the word of a deep cover agent who might or might not be dirty. A deep cover agent who might or might not have told the truth. Excuse me if I don't jump on the *Bull did me a favor* bandwagon because, as far as I know, he could have been the one who shot me."

Jesse had to force himself not to smile. This was the Hanna he'd known before the shooting, and it was good to see her fighting back.

Shaw didn't acknowledge what she'd just said, not verbally anyway, but he stayed quiet, obviously stewing for a couple of long moments. He was still in "glare" mode when he shifted back to Jesse.

"I read your report that Bull called you last night," Shaw said. "Has he contacted you again?"

Jesse wasn't surprised that Shaw had read the report. Grayson would have legally been forced to inform the ATF of the details of the investigation— especially since there was no proof that the ATF had any wrongdoing in this.

"No further contact," Jesse assured the agent. However, he wasn't about to forget what Bull had said.

You need to ask yourself about what really took place that night Hanna was shot.

Jesse had spent a good chunk of the night thinking

about just that, and he still didn't know what Bull had wanted him to figure out. That's why he needed another conversation with Bull, but that wouldn't happen until the man called him back or resurfaced.

"You need to let me know ASAP if you hear from Bull," Shaw said, extracting a business card and handing it to Jesse. "You already have my cell number, but my office number is on there."

"You do the same and let me know if Bull contacts you," Jesse insisted. He didn't have a card on him so he took a notepad from the kitchen counter and jotted down his number.

Shaw took the piece of paper, shoving it into his pocket, and he looked at Hanna again. "I'd appreciate your cooperation in this investigation. If you remember anything, I need you to let me know."

She nodded after a long pause of her own, and that confirmation seemed to signal to Shaw that it was time to leave. He muttered a lukewarm thanks and turned toward the door.

"Don't trust him any further than you can throw a herd of longhorns," Mason muttered as he followed Shaw out of the house.

Good advice; Jesse was on the same page as his uncle. He locked up, reset the security system and looked at Hanna to see if she was about to lose it now that some of her annoyance had faded. Nope. She seemed all-business now.

"You believe anything Shaw said?" she came out and asked.

"Not sure." Hopefully, that would change, and he'd

be able to get some confirmation on things and maybe disprove others. "Are you okay?" He had to know.

She nodded then muttered something under her breath. "I'm very angry that Bull or someone connected to this is putting our baby in danger again."

Jesse matched her nod with one of his own. Yeah, he was not happy about that at all.

"What about Marlene?" Hanna asked. "Is there anything in her background to suggest she could truly be head of the militia?"

"Nothing that jumps out at me, but I suppose it's possible."

Along with interviewing the woman multiple times, Jesse had also done a thorough background check on her. He'd known her for years, but now he tried to determine if everything he remembered added up to her running an illegal operation.

"Both Bull and she were born into money, and Marlene is nearly ten years older than he is," Jesse added. "Their father was a hard man who, from all accounts, browbeat his kids. Bull had a falling out with him and left right after high school. Marlene stayed and, when he died, he left his entire estate to her. It was worth millions, and Marlene has kept the business going though she did move the operation from San Antonio to Silver Creek." That move had happened years ago, right about the time Jesse's mom had married Boone.

"Marlene sells real estate, right?" Hanna asked.

"Yes, and she specializes in commercial property and ranches. I ran financials on her when Bull was arrested. Just routine stuff, and I didn't see any red flags. Still, a real estate business would be a good cover for money laundering and such that a militia might need."

Her forehead bunched up as she obviously tried to process that. "Maybe Bull moved back to Silver Creek to investigate the militia and then found out his sister was involved. That could have possibly caused him to go rogue. Rogue enough, though, to attack and kidnap her? I mean, what reason would Bull have for doing that rather than just turning her over to the ATF?"

He paused, considered it. "Bull might not have taken her. She could have possibly staged the attack in her home. *Possibly*," he emphasized. "It would have involved injuring herself or drawing her own blood."

Even though this was an important and serious conversation, it occurred to him that they hadn't talked like this in a long time. In fact, they hadn't talked much at all since the shooting. It felt good, but he got an instant reminder of just how high the stakes were when he heard Evan's and his mother's laughter coming from the nursery. That's where his focus had to be right now. Keeping Evan safe. Hanna and the rest of his family, too.

"Your shirt had blood on it," Hanna said when Jesse walked back to the kitchen counter where he'd left his laptop.

He stopped, turned and stared at her. "What?"

Hanna swallowed hard. "The first time I saw you. Remember seeing you," she corrected. She motioned toward his chest. "You had blood on your shirt."

He drew in a slow breath. "Yes." Another breath.

"Noah had come running to restrain Bull, so I picked you up and took you to the hospital. I didn't want to wait for the ambulance to get all the way out to the ranch." He paused and blinked hard to try to erase some of what he was reliving in his head. "The baby kicked me."

"What?" she asked, her tone very similar to his just moments earlier.

"When I was running to get you into my truck, you were unconscious, but I could feel Evan kicking. That helped me get through those moments."

She nodded. "You were there with me when they did the C-section?"

He shook his head. "It was an emergency. Medical staff only. But they brought Evan out to me after they cleaned him up." He felt the corner of his mouth lift in an automatic smile. "He was still kicking and crying. He looked like a really-pissed-off hobbit. And in that moment, I knew my life would never be the same."

Hanna smiled, too, because she no doubt knew exactly what he meant. But the smile didn't last. "I heard your mom say something to Boone when I was in the hospital. They were in the room but thought I was asleep. Your mom said you'd had flashbacks of your father's death."

Jesse wanted to curse. He definitely hadn't wanted Hanna to hear something like that when she'd been dealing with her trauma, but yeah, he had had a flashback or two when he'd been trying to save Hanna's life.

"My dad died when I was eight," he said, choosing his words. No need to add more bad images to the ones she no doubt already had. "A car accident. I was with him when a tire blew out and caused him to crash into a tree. I tried to do CPR, but it didn't work."

"Eight," she murmured. Maybe to remind him that he'd been a kid and not responsible. Both of those things were true, but guilt was greedy and apparently had the power to last a lifetime.

"I'm guessing that was one of the things we had in common," Hanna continued. "Because I lost my father when I was young, too. He had a heart attack."

Jesse studied her face. "You remember any of that?"

"No, but my mother told me about it." Her sigh was long and heavy. "And that's the problem. Not specifically with the memories of my father, but the memories of everything. Especially those of when I was attacked."

"'You need to ask yourself about what really took place that night Hanna was shot,'" he said, repeating what Bull had said. Of course, Jesse had to keep considering the theory that Bull could be trying to create some kind of smoke screen, but they wouldn't know until they had a complete picture.

Hanna's memories were a big piece of that picture.

"You recalled me being in your kitchen," Jesse pointed out. "Maybe more will come."

"I could maybe help things along," she said in a murmur, and it seemed to Jesse that she was talking to herself. Trying to steel herself up, too. "I could do hypnosis sessions."

This wasn't the first Jesse was hearing about the

particular therapy that one of Hanna's doctors had suggested. A therapy that she had flat-out rejected. She hadn't spelled out the reason she hadn't wanted to do it, but he suspected she hadn't wanted to deal with the flood of bad memories that would come if the therapy worked.

"I'll call and set up an appointment," Hanna insisted as she took out her phone. But before she could do that, there was the sound of a vehicle in the driveway.

Jesse went on instant alert because he knew if this was someone in his family or from the sheriff's office, he would have gotten a text to notify him.

"Stay back," Jesse warned her, and he went to the window where he saw someone he definitely didn't want to see.

Hanna's mother, Isabel.

The woman wasn't alone. There was a tall, dark-haired man with her, and Isabel was clearly arguing with the deputy, Theo Sheldon who had blocked her from coming closer to the house. Jesse's phone dinged with a text from Miguel Navarro, the ranch hand who was standing guard.

Should we let her in? the ranch hand asked.

"It's your mother," Jesse relayed to Hanna, and that caused her to groan. She groaned a second time when she heard Isabel shout for the deputy to get out of her way, that he couldn't stop her from seeing her daughter.

"She'll have another stroke," Hanna muttered. "Best to let her in."

"She's not alone," Jesse pointed out, causing Hanna to come closer to the window for a quick glance.

"That's Dr. Warner."

Since Jesse was also worried about the woman possibly having another stroke, he responded to Navarro's text. Let her in but search the doctor for any weapons.

That was probably overkill, but Jesse didn't know the man, and he didn't want to take the risk. After all, Bull had had plenty of time to put a plan into motion, a plan that could involve forcing the doctor to help Bull get to them.

Jesse watched as his cousin, Deputy Theo Sheldon, frisked the doctor and then gave Jesse a thumbs-up before he let the pair head for the house. Isabel was obviously spitting mad, but he was surprised at how healthy she looked. He'd seen other stroke victims with limited mobility and serious speech problems, but Isabel was moving just fine. And, judging from her shout at the deputy, she had no trouble talking.

As he'd done with Mason and Agent Shaw, Jesse temporarily disarmed the security system and opened the door. Isabel made it to the porch first and she greeted him with a glare.

"You Rylands can't keep me from my daughter," Isabel added in a snarl.

Dr. Warner didn't protest, but Jesse heard the man's heavy sigh as he followed his patient into the house. Isabel went straight to Hanna and dragged her into her arms.

"How are you holding up? Is the baby okay?" Isabel asked. Coming from her, it sounded like her usual demand.

"We're both fine." Hanna untangled herself from her mother's grip and took a step back. "I told you not to come," she added, aiming that at the doctor.

Dr. Warner lifted his shoulder in a gesture that managed to convey a whole lot of frustration. "Isabel insisted on coming and she was going to drive herself. I opted to bring her for a short visit. Short," he emphasized, aiming a long look at Isabel. "And if she becomes agitated, then I'm taking her right back."

Isabel was already agitated, but she seemed to make an effort to relax her stiff posture. "I just needed to see that my daughter and grandson were okay and to let Hanna know that I'm arranging for some bodyguards. They'll be here within the hour."

Hanna closed her eyes a moment as if fighting to keep her composure. Jesse knew the feeling. He always had to do that around Isabel.

"When the bodyguards arrive, I'll send them away," Hanna informed her mother. "I don't want anyone on the grounds who Jesse hasn't vetted."

Isabel's mouth dropped open and she made a sound of outrage before she whirled around to confront Jesse. "You're trying to control my daughter."

"I'm trying to keep control of the situation," Jesse clarified.

"A situation that wouldn't be happening if you cops had done your job and kept that killer behind bars."

"The cops didn't let Bull escape," Hanna pointed out just as the doctor cautioned her mother.

"Calm down. Now. Or we're leaving."

Dr. Warner took the woman by the arm and led her to the sofa where he had her sit. He got right in her face. "Remember what we talked about on the drive over," he warned her.

"Yes, you threatened to have me dragged back to the rehab facility," Isabel sputtered angrily.

"Not dragged, but taken back," the doctor corrected. "I told you I couldn't stand by and watch you work yourself up into a frenzy. Your meds will only do so much to keep your blood pressure down. You have to do the rest by staying calm. Hanna and your grandson haven't been harmed, and Deputy Ryland here has set up security."

"Security they wouldn't need if the cops had kept that monster where he belongs," Isabel grumbled, but at least she hadn't shouted, and she did seem to be leveling out just a little.

Hanna came into the living room and sat across from her mother. Jesse hoped she wouldn't mention anything about what Shaw had told them or the phone call from Bull. She didn't. Hanna just sat there, staring at her mother, waiting for her to continue. She didn't have to wait long.

"Your studio is gone," Isabel stated. She was definitely calmer now. "How will you work?"

"I've been using the guest room, and I'll keep using it until I can rebuild the studio."

"Or you could just move back to the estate with me where you and Evan would have plenty of room, and you wouldn't be out here all by yourself."

"I'm not moving," Hanna insisted. "I like it here, and the quiet makes it easier for me to paint."

Jesse knew Hanna had felt that way before she'd been shot, and he was always a little surprised to hear she still felt the same. Maybe she didn't need the memories for this place to feel like her home.

"You look different," Isabel volunteered, studying Hanna. "You sound different, too. Is that Jesse's doing—"

"I'm remembering some more things," Hanna interrupted, no doubt cutting off what would have been her mother taking another jab at him.

Isabel pulled back her shoulders, causing Jesse to tune in to the changes in her expression. Not relief or joy. But rather, concern. Maybe because Isabel was worried about the traumatic memories of the shooting?

"More?" Isabel muttered.

"I told you last week that some memories were starting to return," Hanna said. "Bits and pieces."

This was the first Jesse was hearing about that, and he'd seen Hanna at least every other day. Hell. Why had she kept that from him? But he immediately thought of the answer to that. If she'd recalled having sex with him, that probably wasn't something she would feel comfortable spelling out.

"What did you remember?" Isabel asked her after a long pause.

Hanna paused, too. "Some things about Jesse."

So, maybe sex, but after studying Hanna, Jesse thought it might be more than that.

That concern in Isabel's eyes went up a significant notch. "What things about Jesse?" her mother demanded.

Hanna kept her attention nailed to her mother. "Did you tell me you'd make trouble for Jesse if I didn't end my relationship with him?"

What the hell? Jesse definitely hadn't been expecting her to say that. He'd thought Hanna would tell her mother a G-rated version of him in the kitchen the morning after they'd had sex.

Isabel shifted her position and looked away from her daughter. "You remember that?"

"No, I guessed," Hanna admitted. "I figured, with all the other things you'd said about Jesse and his family, that you'd tried to pressure me into not having a relationship with him."

Jesse stared down at Isabel. "What kind of trouble did you plan on causing?" he snapped.

Isabel dodged his gaze as well. "I know people. People like state senator Edgar Lawson."

Since the senator was also the father of one of Silver Creek's deputies, Ava Lawson, Jesse knew the man, too. And didn't think much of him. Many in law enforcement didn't, even though the senator had recently been cleared of having a part in an elaborate money-laundering scheme.

"What exactly did you think the senator would do?" Jesse pressed.

Isabel shrugged again. "Your family runs that huge ranch, and I thought all it would take was a word from Edgar and you wouldn't have buyers lined up for your livestock."

Fat chance of that since the ranch supplied to plenty of people who wouldn't give a rat what the senator thought. Still, it pissed him off that Isabel had threatened his family in any way.

But it had worked.

Well, maybe. Hanna wasn't a pushover, but she might have backed off from him if she'd thought her mother could truly do him or his family some harm.

That could be wishful thinking on his part though.

Jesse would have liked for it to have been something like that, but the truth was that Hanna had been resistant to having a real relationship with him before she'd lost her memory. He'd always thought that might be connected to her broken engagement to Darrin Madison, the son of one of Isabel's close friends, but that might not have played into it either. The bottom line was that Hanna hadn't loved him and hadn't wanted the marriage he'd offered for the sake of their baby.

Isabel groaned, causing Jesse's attention to snap back to her. He was both shocked and confused when he saw the tears in her eyes. "I asked Marlene to help. Hanna had already stopped seeing you, but I was worried she might change her mind and go back to you. I couldn't live with that, not after the way your family tried to ruin my life."

Jesse had to do a mental double take, and he cut through the bulk of the woman's confession to home in on one important point. "Marlene? Bull's sister?"

The woman nodded. "We travel in some of the same social circles, and we've been friendly for years. The last time I saw her, I mentioned that I wasn't happy about my daughter being involved with a Ryland. She must have seen how upset I was, and she said that maybe there was something she could do to help."

Everything inside Jesse went still. "When did this happen? When did Marlene tell you she could help?"

Isabel made a hoarse sob. "The day before Hanna was shot. Oh, God." She pressed her fingers to her mouth. "Do you think Marlene is the one who persuaded her brother into going to the ranch to confront you? Am I responsible for nearly getting Hanna and Evan killed?"

Chapter Six

Hanna set Evan's bottle aside and eased across the room to put him in his crib for his morning nap. Even though it was obvious he was already asleep and would likely stay that way for an hour or more, she stood there watching him. Just seeing her baby had a way of steadying her.

And scaring her, too.

Her precious little boy was in danger because of Jesse and her. Because someone might want to silence them, and she might have her mother to blame for the start of that.

Shortly after Isabel had dropped her bombshell that she might have spurred the shooting, Dr. Warner had convinced her that it was time to leave. Isabel had, crying her way out the door, and Hanna hadn't been able to force herself to offer any consolation. If Isabel had indeed had a part in what had happened, Hanna wasn't sure she could ever forgive her.

Hanna darn sure didn't expect Jesse or his family to forgive her either. Isabel had crossed one very big line, and it didn't matter that the woman hadn't known what the consequences would be. The bottom line was she'd put Evan and her at risk. Her actions could have cost Jesse and her their son.

Hanna went back into the kitchen where she found Jesse exactly where she'd left him a half hour earlier, before she'd gone to the nursery to feed Evan and put him down for his nap. He was sitting at the kitchen counter, working on his laptop while he drank yet another cup of coffee.

"My mother already left," Jesse let her know. "One of the ranch hands came and picked her up."

That was good. While she truly appreciated Melissa's help with Evan while Jesse and she had been dealing with Shaw and then Isabel, Hanna had needed some quiet time with her son. Of course, Jesse was here, too, in the middle of that quietness, but it felt different with him.

Was different, she silently amended.

For the first time since the shooting, it seemed as if Jesse and she were on the same side. Then again, maybe that "same side" had been there before she'd lost her memory. That was the problem with this messy situation. What she didn't know, or remember, could be just as dangerous as her getting back her entire memory.

"I got a text from Dr. Warner while I was feeding Evan," Hanna told him, setting the baby monitor on the counter so she could keep an eye on Evan. "He has my mother back at the rehab facility. He said he'd given her a mild sedative because she was still upset."

Jesse turned, looked at her. "Are *you* still upset?"

There was no reason to hold back the truth on this. "Yes, and you should be as well."

Her mother's words just wouldn't stop repeating in her head. *Am I responsible for nearly getting Hanna and Evan killed?* It was definitely a question that needed answering.

"It was a good guess on your part that your mother would try to keep you away from me by threatening my family," Jesse remarked. "It was a guess, right?"

Hanna nodded, got a glass of water and leaned against the counter to face him. "But I don't remember if what my mom said had any impact on my decision not to accept your marriage proposal. Or to end things with you."

He opened his mouth, closed it, and seemed to have a debate with himself as to what to say. "You told me there was no relationship to end, that it was only a one-night deal between us."

She winced, hoping it hadn't been as hurtful as it sounded. But according to what Jesse had told her, it had indeed been just one night. One that'd left her pregnant. She'd never come out and asked Jesse why that had happened, but in one of their brief conversations after the shooting, she had brought up the pregnancy, and he'd mentioned that he had used a condom. So, they'd practiced safe sex. For all the good it'd done.

Except there was plenty of good when she considered she now had her son.

That was playing into this messy situation, too. Jesse was Evan's father. Always would be. And she didn't have to actually remember being with him to know what had drawn her to him. Then and now. The attraction, yes. But more. She knew in her gut that Jesse was a good man. One who her mother had tried to give a raw deal because of the bitterness she felt toward his family.

"You said you told your mother about a week ago that you were getting back bits and pieces of your memory." Jesse threw it out there.

"A lie," Hanna readily admitted. "I thought it would make her stop worrying. Or at least worry less about me. I didn't want her to lose hope that I'd make a full recovery, so I told her I was remembering some things."

In hindsight, that hadn't worked. Maybe nothing would. But that hadn't stopped her from trying to soothe Isabel and perhaps dole out some hope to herself, as well, that she wouldn't permanently stay in the dark when it came to all those missing years and memories of her life.

"A couple of days ago, I was going through all my old emails and texts, just to see if there was anything that would jog my memory," she told Jesse. "Did you or Grayson take a look at those?"

He shook his head. "You were a victim and not target-specific. At least, that's what we believed." His face tightened. "Were we wrong about that?"

"No," she tried to assure him. "I didn't find threats or anything like that. Definitely nothing from Bull, Marlene, Arnie, or anyone else with obvious connections to the militia or the attack." She paused. Had to. "I found some texts, though, from Darrin Madison."

Even though Darrin didn't live in Silver Creek, Jesse no doubt knew that was the name of her ex-fiancé. She was also betting the town's rumor mill had been plenty busy with gossip about their breakup. Darrin was an investment mogul who had the added bonus of being a Texas heartthrob.

Among other things.

She had ended their engagement a little less than two years ago and, five months later, she'd landed in bed with Jesse. Maybe for rebound sex. Perhaps because the attraction had simply been that strong between them. But even without her memories, those texts had given her some insight.

"He hit me," she heard herself say.

Jesse jerked back as if someone had punched him. He cursed under his breath, shook his head and then cursed some more. "I'm sorry. I hope he paid and paid hard for that."

Hanna couldn't be sure, but she doubted that he had. "I broke up with him, but he wasn't arrested because I didn't report it," she admitted. "I can read through the lines of the flurry of texts from him and my mother. Darrin went into the groveling 'but you caused me to do it' mode. He insisted I made him snap when I accused him of having an affair with his assistant. He was having an affair, by the way. He finally admitted that in one of the texts."

"And what the hell did Isabel say about it?" Jesse snapped.

Hanna managed a dry smile. "She thought I should forgive him and get counseling so I didn't trigger Darrin into another impulsive gesture. *Impulsive gesture*," she emphasized. "Those are the words Isabel used." She shook her head. "I'm betting there were a lot of phone calls and visits to try to pressure me into getting back with him."

"Did he pressure you too?" Jesse asked, the anger still biting in his voice.

"It seems that he did. According to the texts, he sent flowers, asked me to go on a romantic getaway so we could work things out, etcetera. I turned down all his offers, and then I stopped responding. He eventually stopped, too, and moved on. Isabel mentioned he recently got engaged again."

He studied her face, maybe looking for any signs that bothered her. It didn't. "I dodged a bullet with him." Then, she wanted to kick herself for phrasing it that way. "Sorry. Not an especially good reference, considering I didn't dodge the one Arnie fired. Or maybe it was Bull who pulled the trigger."

Her voice cracked a little on those last words and, for a second, she was right back in the hospital. In pain, terrified and with the panic swelling inside her because she couldn't remember what the heck had happened.

That crack in her voice and her troubled expression was probably why Jesse slid his hand over hers. For just a moment. Then he pulled back, which was normally something she would do. For just this one time, though, she wished he'd kept the contact there a little longer.

It was wrong to take comfort from him. Wrong to give him any kind of hope that she'd ever consider the marriage proposal he had told her would always be on the table.

"I still want to set up an appointment for hypnosis," she said. "But..."

"But even if you get your memory back, you might not want a relationship with me. Or with anyone. In fact, remembering might make things worse in that area. I get that." He stopped and looked her straight in the eyes. "FYI, I want to beat your ex to a pulp for hitting you."

She mentally compared that to her mother's reaction, and it touched her. So many emotions welled up inside her, and they collided with the fear and uncertainty. Maybe that's why she took those steps toward him. And why she went into his arms when he reached for her.

Her body landed on his and Hanna could feel herself melting against him. Now, this was what she needed. The close contact. Being in his arms with his scent right there for her to take in. He was strong, so strong, with the muscles corded in his chest and biceps. And while he would respect her no-marriage wish, she had a clear sense that he still cared for her.

So that's why she pulled back.

"Sorry," she muttered just as Jesse said, "Don't say you're sorry."

"You're shaken up," he continued a moment later. "You have a right to be shaken up."

She did, but playing with fire wouldn't help, and that's what she would be doing if she'd stayed in his arms. Scalding-hot fire that had led to sex once and could again if she wasn't careful. She was in no position whatsoever to allow that to happen.

"The investigation…" she said, forcing herself to change the subject. "Have you found anything that'll help?"

Jesse kept his eyes on her for a while longer. Perhaps because he was trying to decide whether to go with the new topic or linger on that hug that shouldn't have happened. Thankfully, he went with the first.

"I haven't been able to confirm that Bull is or isn't an agent," Jesse explained. "I don't know if I can trust Shaw, which means I don't know if he told us the truth. It's possible Bull is just his criminal informant. Possible, too, that Shaw's worked out some kind of deal with Bull to get him info on the militia so he can get the credit for taking it down."

Hanna imagined that would give Agent Shaw a stellar mark on his record, if he closed such a big case. The agent might go to any lengths to make that happen.

"A deal with Bull that Shaw's possibly kept off the books?" she asked.

Jesse nodded. "But it could be worse than that. A lot worse."

Hanna knew where he was going with this. "Shaw

could be dirty and want to silence me before my memory returns."

Another nod. "And maybe he needs to silence Bull, too. Or anybody else who could prove he's dirty."

Yes, and that would include Jesse. With all the digging he was doing, Shaw had to know that something might be uncovered that he could want to stay hidden.

"Of course, there's the possibility that Shaw's clean and that Bull actually is a deep cover agent," Jesse went on. "If so, that means Marlene could be the criminal in all of this."

"Are there any signs that's possible?" Hanna wanted to know.

"There are a few flags. Not bright red ones, but still flags." Jesse went back to his laptop and looked at the screen. Hanna took a glance at it, too, and realized Jesse had a financial report on the woman.

Hanna zoomed right into one particular bit of info. "Marlene has an offshore account."

"She does, and while that's not automatically illegal, it makes me wonder why she'd need something like that. Of course, it's possible someone else set up the account without her knowledge."

True. Because if Marlene had wanted to hide funds she'd gotten from the militia, then why use her own name? Then again, maybe the woman had thought the cops wouldn't look that deep into her background.

"Her local bank account and investments look normal enough," Jesse went on, "but since she buys and sells real estate, there's always ways to conceal things like money laundering or the purchase of weapons and such." He looked up from the screen and met her gaze. "She did business with your mother, sold her some land and worked with her to get tax breaks on some of the property she already owned."

"Isabel never mentioned that," Hanna muttered, "and she would have had the perfect opening to do that when you asked her about Marlene."

Her mother had said they were in the same *social circle* and were *friendly*. Nothing about doing business with the woman who might be a criminal.

Jesse made a sound of agreement, but his attention whipped to his phone when he got a text. "It's Theo," he told her, and he started toward the door.

Theo Sheldon. Another deputy in the Silver Creek sheriff's office and a Ryland relative. Well, sort of. From what Hanna had gathered from the bits and pieces of talk she'd heard from Isabel and others, Theo's parents had been murdered when he was a kid, and he'd been raised by Grayson and his wife. If the other talk she'd heard was true, then Theo was the top candidate to replace Grayson as sheriff when he retired in a couple of months.

She stayed back, away from the door and windows, something Jesse had drilled into her, and watched as Jesse ushered in his fellow deputy. Unlike the dark-haired Rylands, Theo was blond, but he still had the cop's eyes.

"Hanna," Theo greeted while Jesse locked up. "We haven't found Bull or Marlene yet," he volunteered, probably because he knew that Hanna was about to ask that particular question. "No sightings of either of them."

Part of her hoped they were long gone and were now out of the state. Especially Bull. But that would be just a different kind of nightmare since she would always be looking over her shoulder to see if he had returned to finish the job he'd started. No. It was best for the cops to find him and figure out what the heck had actually happened when she'd been shot.

"I've been going through Marlene's financials," Jesse explained. "I highlighted some areas that need more digging. Any luck with her phone records?"

"Possibly," Theo answered. "She had no calls to or from the prison, but she did get two from an unknown caller shortly after Bull's escape. They were both very short, only lasting a couple of seconds, which means she could have realized they were spam and ended them."

Jesse nodded. "True. Is there a pattern of her getting calls from anyone who might be connected to Bull or the militia?"

"No, but I figure she'd use burners for that so they couldn't be traced." Theo paused, shifted his attention to Hanna. "Marlene did get calls from your mother. One the day before you were shot and two more the day after."

That tightened her stomach into a hard knot. "They were long conversations?"

"Long," Theo verified. "The one before the shooting lasted nearly a half hour. I'll need to go to the rehab facility in San Antonio to talk to your mother about exactly what was said during those calls."

He wasn't asking permission, and Hanna hadn't expected him to do that. The interview needed to be done, and Isabel had to come clean with what she knew. Hanna also thought of something else that should happen, something that might give them a few answers.

"My phone kept a record of my texts for the past year, but there are only two months of calls," she explained. "I'm wondering if someone can access those earlier calls, the ones I received prior to the shooting, to see if any of them…well, are unusual. If there are any flags."

That obviously got both Theo's and Jesse's attention. "You mean something like Marlene contacting you? Or Bull?" Jesse prompted.

She nodded then shrugged. Then sighed. "Maybe it's nothing. I mean, we know why I came to the ranch that night. I had ultrasound pictures and forms from the hospital in the car with me, and I'd told the nurse that I would take them out to you right away to get them signed, but maybe there was another reason I was there—"

"I'll have your calls checked," Jesse assured her, and he took out his phone to fire off a text that would get that started.

"Just how fragile is your mom's health?" Theo asked her while Jesse finished his text. "Because I need to know how much I can push to get answers."

"She seemed physically fine when she was here

earlier, but go through Dr. Warner," she suggested. "Maybe even have him present during the questioning. He can perhaps keep her calm."

Of course, he could also put a stop to the interview if Isabel became too agitated, but they couldn't risk bringing on another stroke. Even if her mother had done something to instigate the shooting, she had indeed had a stroke, and a second one might be a lot more serious. It could kill her. Hanna didn't want that. However, if Isabel had played even a small part in what had happened, she expected her to have to pay for that in some way.

And maybe she had.

Hanna didn't doubt that Isabel loved Evan, and it was probably eating away at her to know that she'd inadvertently put her grandson and daughter in harm's way. She had possibly done that anyway, but it was just as likely that Marlene had been blowing smoke with her *something she could do to help.*

"Grayson got the crime lab to go through another enhancement of the footage from the security camera the night of the shooting," Theo went on. "It's ready if you want to take a look at it."

It took Hanna a moment to realize Theo had meant that offer for both Jesse and her. She had to swallow hard and tamp down the blasted panic. Not now. This could be important, critical to getting to the truth, and that's why she nodded.

"Yes, I'd like to see it," she attested.

But Jesse didn't budge. "You've looked at the enhanced footage?" he asked his cousin.

Theo shook his head. "It just came in a half hour ago. You can access it through the online case file."

His gaze stayed on Jesse and something unspoken passed between them. Hanna was betting it had to do with her. Theo probably thought it a good idea for Jesse to review the footage to make sure it was something she could handle.

"I'll take a look at it then," Jesse muttered.

She heard what he wasn't saying. That he would look at it and decide if it was something she should see. But Hanna didn't want him making a decision like that for her. She couldn't risk Jesse trying to shield her from something that could help them uncover the truth.

Theo nodded, sliding glances at both Jesse and her before he continued. "Agent Shaw came by the sheriff's office after he left here." He was obviously moving on to the rest of the updates he'd planned on giving Jesse. "He's still pushing to get Hanna put in protective custody."

"Push back," Jesse advised.

"Oh, we are. The ATF has no jurisdiction when it comes to Hanna or Evan. Shaw can squawk all he wants, but he can't change that."

"Any indications that Shaw's dirty?" Hanna came out and asked.

Theo shrugged. "Not dirty, but he toes the line a lot. He's had two complaints filed against him for excessive force, and there's talk that he's bent the law a couple of times. Nothing to do with Bull or the militia, but it's possible Shaw's done unauthorized wire taps to get info on an investigation."

That didn't help the knot in her stomach, and Hanna frantically tried to recall if Agent Shaw had had the chance to plant a bug in her house.

"Shaw was never out of my sight when he was here," Jesse assured her. Obviously, he knew where her thoughts had gone. "And he was only in this room, nowhere else in the house. But I can have the place swept just in case."

Hanna nodded. She didn't want to risk the chance that a dirty ATF agent could be listening in on their conversations—both the ones that dealt with the investigation and those that were personal.

"I'm heading to San Antonio now to talk with Isabel, but I can schedule the sweep on the drive there," Theo offered, checking the time. "We're having the sheriff's office swept, too, just in case Shaw's trying to get an inside line on what we're doing." He glanced around. "In the meantime, if there is a bug, you two might not want to have any conversations in here."

"Good idea," Jesse muttered, and he walked with Theo to the door.

Once he'd locked back up, he grabbed his laptop and said, "Why don't we move to the guest room to finish looking at Marlene's financials?"

She nodded, nabbing her water and the baby monitor so she could follow him. This was the right thing to do, but Hanna knew it would be a little unnerving to be in a bedroom with Jesse. That hug sure hadn't helped in that department. Then again, she hadn't needed that hug to recall just how attracted she was to him.

"And the enhanced footage from the surveillance camera?" she asked.

He sighed in such a way that let her know he hadn't just expected her to drop that. "It could help if I view it first because there might be nothing new to see." The moment he finished saying that, though, he waved it off. "But there might be something new for you to see."

"Yes," she agreed, and she left it at that.

She watched Jesse try to deal with the dilemma, torn between sheltering her and using her. "Yes," he finally repeated. "We'll do that after we finish with Marlene's financials. I don't want to skip any steps here."

Neither did she, and that's why Hanna wanted to study those financial records, too. She didn't need memories to maybe clue in to something that just didn't seem right.

Jesse carried his laptop into the guest room and he'd just set it up when his phone rang. The sound shot through the room and frayed her nerves even more than they already were.

"Unknown caller," he told her after he glanced at the screen. "I'm going to put it on speaker." He also hit the record function on his phone.

"It's me," the caller said. Bull Freeman.

"Where the hell are you?" Jesse asked.

"Nearby. We need to meet."

"Why?" Jesse snarled. "So you can try to kill me?"

"No, so I can turn myself in. Meet me at the fence of that old, abandoned farm out on Franklin Road."

Hanna had no idea where that was, but she was betting it was a remote location. The perfect place for Bull to lie in wait and try to gun Jesse down.

"I suppose you expect me to be alone and unarmed?" The sarcasm was heavy in Jesse's voice.

"No," Bull repeated. "You can bring your fellow lawmen and an entire arsenal with you. Just be there in two hours."

"If you're nearby, like you say, why do you need so much time?" Jesse argued.

"Because I've got some things to do." Bull paused, cursed. "I'm putting my life in your hands, Jesse. Don't do something that'll get us both killed."

Chapter Seven

Jesse listened to the chatter of the conference call with Grayson, Deputy Ava Lawson and Texas Ranger Harley Ryland. They were going over the same map that Jesse had pulled up on his laptop.

The map of the area where Bull had insisted he would surrender himself.

Jesse had serious doubts about Bull's intentions, but that wouldn't stop him from going to the abandoned farm. However, he would do that with plenty of backup and security measures.

One of the best measures was Harley himself because he was an expert sniper. And Grayson was placing Harley in the loft of the barn on the farm. During the past hour since Bull had called, Grayson had already had a team check out the barn and surrounding area for booby traps and such.

Grayson had also made other arrangements in that same hour. There'd be deputies in the wooded area across from the farm. The road to and from there would be monitored as well. Everyone would wear Kevlar, and Jesse wouldn't be exiting the bullet-resistant cruiser until Bull had assumed a position of surrender.

"It's still not foolproof," Jesse heard Hanna murmur.

She was watching the baby monitor since it was nearing the time for Evan to wake from his nap, but she was obviously listening to the conversation as well. Hard for her not to hear it, though, considering the small size of the guest room.

"It'll be as safe as we can possibly make it," Jesse assured her in a whisper.

That, of course, wasn't foolproof at all.

Bull could have assembled his own team who would try to kill every lawman on scene. He wouldn't be able to have that team in the immediate area since Grayson already had deputies posted there, but Bull's cronies could come storming in by using the trails.

But Bull could have something else in mind.

Something that was twisting Jesse up inside.

Because Bull could be planning a different kind of attack. One where he would use this so-called surrender as a diversion so he could come after Hanna. Jesse had tried to cover all the angles there, too, by arranging for more than a dozen armed ranch hands to be on the grounds. That was in addition to having his uncle Mason and cousin Noah and two more reserve deputies there as well.

Jesse's mother would be inside the house with Hanna and Evan, and because Melissa was a former cop, she would be armed with a gun that she most definitely knew how to use. His mother would lay down her life to protect Hanna and Evan, and yeah, that was twisting him up, too. He didn't want it to come down to his mom having to step in to assist because it would mean Bull and whoever he'd brought with him had managed to get past multiple lines of defense.

"Any questions?" Grayson asked when he finished the briefing.

No one said anything. Grayson had made clear everyone's positions. Had made it equally clear that they wouldn't be giving Bull any chance to fire at any of them. They also wouldn't be letting Agent Shaw in on it. Too risky, since the man could be dirty.

Jesse ended the call and checked the time. "I'll have to leave in about an hour," he told her.

He also checked Hanna to see how she was handling this. She didn't seem to be on the verge of a panic attack, nowhere close to that, but her nerves were definitely showing. Even though he wasn't even sure it would help, he went to her and pulled her into his arms again.

"It'll be okay," he tried to assure her. Of course, they knew it wasn't something he could guarantee, but he would do whatever it took to keep them all safe. Bull was the expendable one here.

Hanna didn't move away from him, and she didn't go stiff from the close contact. The sigh that left her mouth was long and laced with fear and worry.

"You think Bull will actually surrender?" she asked.

"I don't know," he answered honestly.

It could go either way. If the man was truly an

ATF agent, a clean one, then the chances were high that he'd give himself up. He would want to clear his name. But if he was truly a killer or a dirty agent, then all bets were off.

She nodded, her hair brushing against the side of his face. That gave him a kick of memories he didn't want at the moment. Memories not of the damage that Bull could do but of Hanna and him together. Oh, man. Even with everything that'd happened, she could still fire up his body and make him remember things best put on hold.

Obviously, they were on the same page about that "on hold" part because she cleared her throat and stepped back. Her gaze automatically went to the monitor where she could see that Evan was still sleeping.

"I'm not sure how soon he'll be waking up," she said, her voice a low murmur, "but I can go ahead and start looking at that enhanced feed from the security camera that Theo mentioned."

That yanked him out of the haze from the heat, and Jesse couldn't shake his head fast enough. "I don't want you to have to deal with that now. Like I said, I have to leave in about an hour. If you see something that upsets you or triggers a panic attack, I want to be here." And it might take more than the hour to get her steady.

"I want to get started on this." She paused, and he could see her mentally regroup. "I *need* to get started on it. I need to do something to help so I don't just feel like a victim who needs protection. If we can put an end to the danger, then Evan will be safe."

Jesse couldn't dispute any of that, but the timing sucked. He'd seen that footage. Not the enhanced, but the original one. Hell, he'd studied it frame by frame, and he knew it was going to bring all that terror back for her. For him, too.

"I won't fall apart," she assured him. "I can't because I need to take care of Evan when he wakes up."

She would definitely need to do that, and their little boy could be the ultimate, good distraction. Still, he debated it for another moment before he finally went to his laptop and located the file in his inbox. He had Hanna sit in the chair, and he pressed the keys to get the footage started.

At first glance, Jesse couldn't see much of a difference in the enhanced footage in the first few frames. He watched as Hanna pulled to a stop in front of the gate and then opened her window to punch in the security code Jesse had given her. However, before she could do that, Arnie's truck came to a fast stop behind her, and both Arnie and Bull barreled out, heading straight for the gate.

Or maybe Hanna's car.

Because of the angle of the camera, Jesse couldn't see Hanna's expression, but at that moment, she wouldn't have necessarily been scared. The men didn't have weapons drawn. Not yet. But Jesse was betting the terror came and skyrocketed for her once she saw the rage on Arnie's face.

Jesse adjusted his own position so he could see both the laptop screen and the side of Hanna's face. That way, he could stop this if things got too intense.

Better yet, maybe Evan would go ahead and wake up so it'd put an end to this. A temporary end anyway. Jesse knew that eventually Hanna would see every second of what the camera had captured.

"This appears to be when things escalated," Hanna muttered as she continued to watch.

Yeah, it was, and she was referring to the fact that she'd reached out of her window to punch in the code to open the gate. Arnie had stopped her from doing that by throwing open the passenger's-side door of her car, and then the man had taken hold of her.

The lab had indeed enhanced these frames. They'd managed to lighten the footage and make it clearer. Too clear. Jesse felt a wave of rage all over again when Arnie freed Hanna of her seat belt and dragged her out from the passenger's side. He'd had to do that because the metal post with the security pad would have prevented him from getting her out on the driver's side since she'd parked right next to it so she could reach it.

"We had no luck getting lip readers to interpret what's being said," Jesse explained. But Arnie was clearly agitated, and it appeared he was yelling at both Hanna and Bull.

"I'm not going to focus on my own face," she told him in a ragged whisper. "That probably won't help."

Probably not. Though he wasn't sure it would help for her to look at Arnie's and Bull's faces, either, but that's what she did. She leaned closer to the screen, watching and focusing.

They watched Arnie hook his arm around her

throat once he had Hanna out of her car. He still had his truck keys in that same hand, and they dangled from his fingers, hitting against Hanna's neck. Arnie took a few steps back before he whipped out a gun and started dragging Hanna toward his truck. Bull sure as hell hadn't tried to stop him. Not physically, anyway, but the men continued to talk.

Maybe even argue.

Jesse saw Arnie drop the truck keys. Hanna had been the reason for that because she'd been struggling to get away from him. Arnie had lost his grip on the keys and they'd fallen into the grass and shrubs lining the road. That obviously hadn't pleased the man, and his face had tightened with even more rage.

"There were drugs in his system," Jesse told her even though that was something she had no doubt already heard. Arnie had been stoned on a cocktail of alcohol and cocaine.

She shook her head. "I wish I could remember what he was saying. That's key. I have to remember."

Key was the right word, but it was possible she might never recover those memories. Hell, if seeing this didn't trigger the recovery, then maybe nothing would. Maybe not even the hypnosis. If that turned out to be the case, then that meant they'd have to pick through Bull's version of events to figure out what the heck had actually happened.

Jesse braced himself for the final frames, and he watched Arnie's wild eyes home in on the security camera. The drugs and booze obviously hadn't affected his aim because he lifted his gun and fired the shot to blast the camera to smithereens.

Hanna released a long breath and sat back in the chair. "I can keep watching it to see if I notice anything that'll help."

Jesse was about to nix that, but his phone rang and he saw Noah's name on the screen. An uneasy feeling slammed through him. Maybe something had gone wrong with the plan to meet Bull.

"What happened?" Jesse immediately asked.

"I'm here with your mother, but another car just pulled up," Noah explained. "It's Marlene."

Of all the things Jesse had expected his cousin to say, that wasn't one of them. "Marlene," he repeated. He saw the surprise that was on Hanna's face as well. "She's alive then. Is she hurt?"

"She appears to have a head injury, but she won't let me come near the car. She says she'll drive off if I get closer. She wants to talk to Hanna."

Jesse groaned then cursed. "That's not going to happen. Go ahead and bring my mother inside the house. I'll call for backup and then try to talk to Marlene myself."

Hanna quickly shook her head. "You can't go out there. It could be a trap."

Possibly, but he was a cop and he had to do his job. Marlene could be either a suspect or a key witness, and he needed to find out which.

Jesse headed to the front door and Hanna was right behind him after she grabbed the baby monitor. He got his mom and Noah inside and then looked out the window. It was Marlene all right. She was behind the wheel of a beat-up white car, and Jesse could see the blood on the side of her head.

"Is Evan okay?" his mom immediately asked.

Hanna nodded. "But he'll be up from his nap any minute now."

"I'll go to the nursery then, so I can be there when he wakes up." His mom gave both their arms a reassuring pat before she started down the hall.

While Jesse continued to keep his eyes on Marlene, he called for an ambulance. He knew Noah wouldn't have any trouble being his backup, and with so many of the deputies tied up, Jesse didn't want to call Grayson for help.

Once he was done with his call, he motioned for Hanna to stay back. When he was certain she was as safe as he could manage, he opened the door a fraction. He also drew his gun, but he kept it down by the side of his leg. Out of sight but ready in case things turned ugly.

"Marlene," Jesse called out. "How badly are you hurt?"

"I need to talk to Hanna," the woman answered, obviously dodging his question. She started and ended her response with loud sobs.

Sobs that could be fake, Jesse reminded himself, and injuries that could be staged. With the flags in her financials, Jesse couldn't just blindly trust her. However, he did have to secure the situation before the ambulance arrived.

"I need you to get out of the car," Jesse instructed. "And keep your hands where I can see them."

That brought on more sobs and what he thought was a yell filled with outrage. "I need to see Hanna. I have to tell her what happened."

"You can tell me." In contrast, Jesse kept his voice calm. "Just get out of the car, so I can help you."

The woman didn't budge, but he did see her pick up something. His hand tensed on his gun, but he didn't aim. Not yet. He watched and saw that it was a phone. It was some long snail-crawling moments before his own phone rang. From Dispatch. When Marlene motioned for him to answer it, he realized she wouldn't have had his number, but the call could have been routed to him through the emergency operator.

Without taking his attention off Marlene, Jesse hit the answer function with his left thumb and put the call on speaker.

"Please," Marlene begged. "Let me speak to Hanna."

Jesse wasn't ready to do that just yet. Besides, Hanna would no doubt be able to hear what was said.

"Did Bull hurt you?" Jesse asked the woman.

"Hanna?" Marlene shouted. "Please. I need to tell you something."

Jesse considered pressing Marlene for more info, but her crying had gotten even louder, and he could see the blood on the side of her head had started to trickle down her cheek.

"Hanna won't be going outside," Jesse told her so he could set the ground rules. "Tell her what you have to say and then let the EMTs help you. The ambulance will be here in a couple of minutes."

"No," Marlene shouted. "She'll have them kill me if she gets the chance."

Jesse had to mentally replay that. Marlene sure as hell had better not be talking about Hanna. "She?" he challenged.

But again, Marlene didn't answer his question. "I can't go to the hospital," she insisted. "She'll have her goons get to me. She'll try to silence me."

"No one will try to silence you. Detective Noah Ryland is here, and he can go in the ambulance with you to the hospital." He paused a moment to see if Marlene would have any objections to that. She didn't voice them if she did. "Now, tell me who this *she* is that you're so scared of."

This time the sound was more than a sob, and Marlene wailed out her answer. "Isabel. It's Hanna's mother who tried to kill me."

Chapter Eight

Hanna stood back from the window, but she was still able to see the EMTs loading Marlene into the ambulance. Noah was right there beside the woman and, judging from his body language, he was trying to keep her calm.

Trying and failing.

Marlene was crying and still going on about Isabel trying to kill her. Hanna didn't believe her. *Couldn't* believe her. Isabel wasn't exactly in a position to kidnap or hurt someone, but that hadn't stopped Hanna from calling her mother to try and get to the bottom of Marlene's accusation.

A call that'd gone straight to voice mail.

It was the same for the one she'd then made to Dr. Warner. It was only after multiple attempts to reach both of them that Hanna remembered they might still be in the interview with Theo. If so, they'd hopefully see that she had tried to contact them and would get back to her right away.

Jesse finished his call with Grayson, but before she could ask if Theo knew about Marlene showing up at her place, his phone rang again. "It's one of the EMTs," Jesse informed her.

He'd yet to shut and lock the door and was keeping watch, no doubt to make sure Marlene and his cousin weren't attacked. Even with the ten feet or so distance between Jesse and her, she had no trouble hearing the EMT when he spoke.

"I think she's been drugged," he told Jesse. "Can't confirm it, of course, but they'll run tests at the hospital."

Drugged. That might account for Marlene's confusion about who'd kidnapped her.

"What are her injuries?" Jesse asked.

"The most obvious one is the head wound," the EMT immediately answered. "It looks as if someone bashed her pretty hard, and she might have a concussion. Other than that, she has bruises and abrasions on her wrists and ankles, and some of those abrasions are fairly deep."

So, she had likely been tied up and held somewhere, if the woman's story was to be believed. The injuries could also be self-inflicted, but that seemed extreme for a fake kidnapping. A head wound could be serious—as Hanna well knew.

"Noah is to stay with Marlene at all times," Jesse reminded the EMT. "Once she's at the hospital, a deputy will come over and stand guard. I want her clothes bagged and her fingernails checked for any traces of DNA. I also don't want anyone other than medical personnel and law enforcement to talk to her, understand? If someone tries, have the deputy intervene."

"Got it," the EMT assured him before they ended the call.

Jesse checked his watch, something he'd been doing a lot in the past hour, and it was a reminder that even with all of this happening, he needed to leave soon for his meeting with Bull. He obviously had way too much on his mind, but that didn't stop him from going to her after he locked the door and reset the security.

He ran his hand down the length of her arm and took hold of her hand, intertwining his fingers with hers. "Since Noah might be tied up with Marlene for a while, Grayson is having Deputy Ava Lawson come here to help keep watch."

Hanna shook her head. "But she's supposed to be at the abandoned farm with you and the others."

"A reserve deputy will take her place," he explained.

Obviously, Jesse figured an actual deputy would do a better job than a reserve one, which meant he was at greater risk for his meeting with Bull. A risk because he wanted the actual deputy here. Hanna wanted to argue with that, wanted Jesse to have that extra level of security, but she also knew their top priority was to keep Evan safe. Even if that put Jesse, or her, at greater risk.

"Thank you," she muttered. "Thank you for everything."

She tried not to show the worry since he was in that "full-plate worry" mode already, but he was well aware of what was on her mind.

"The person who kidnapped Marlene might have

tricked her into thinking Isabel was behind this," Jesse suggested.

Since it was something Hanna had considered just moments earlier, she nodded. But the possibility of her mother's involvement was still weighing her down like heavy stones. "When do you have to leave?"

"I've got a few minutes. I figured I'd pop into the nursery and see Evan. Is he awake?"

"Yes." She showed him the monitor she still had so he could see his mother holding Evan in the rocking chair while she read to him. Soon, very soon, she'd need to fix him lunch, but since he wasn't fussing, it could wait until after Jesse had had those few minutes with him.

They started for the nursery but this time it was Hanna's phone that rang. She let out a breath of relief when she saw it was Dr. Warner.

"I just want you to know that we're doing everything possible to find your mother," the doctor said the moment she answered.

Hanna had put the call on speaker so, obviously, Jesse had heard that loud and clear. "What do you mean find her?" he asked just as his own phone rang. He cursed when Theo's name popped up, and he stepped aside to take the call.

"Dr. Warner, what happened to my mother?" Hanna demanded. She had to speak through the tight grip her muscles now had on her throat.

"She left the facility. She didn't tell anyone," he quickly added. "She just left."

Hanna resisted the urge to curse and forced herself to stay calm. "When did this happen and why? Was she upset with Deputy Sheldon's interview?"

"The deputy didn't even see her. When he got here, the nurse called Isabel's room, and Isabel said she was just getting dressed, to give her a few minutes. After those minutes dragged on, I went to check on her, and she wasn't there. We went through the footage on the security cameras and we spotted her leaving. She went to the parking lot, got in her car and drove away."

"Drove away in the car that shouldn't have been there," Hanna snarled under her breath. Again, she had to fight to hang on to her composure, and judging from the snippets she was hearing of Jesse's conversation with Theo, he wasn't hearing happy news either.

"Is my mother actually capable of driving?" Hanna asked.

"She's done very well with her exercises and has regained nearly all of the mobility she had before the stroke. Her response times might not be as quick, though, since she hasn't driven in a while."

And that was a huge reason for concern. "Has Deputy Sheldon alerted the San Antonio PD?"

"He has, and I'm sure they'll find her. He's also sending someone to her house in Silver Creek in case she goes there."

Good, so Theo was covering all the bases. Still, it was beyond frustrating, especially considering the accusation Marlene had made.

"Has a woman named Marlene Freeman ever visited my mother there at the facility?" Hanna asked.

"The name's not familiar, but I can check the visitors' log," the doctor offered. "You think this woman had something to do with your mother leaving?"

Hanna settled for making a noncommittal sound. She didn't know how her mother could have found out what Marlene was claiming, but it was possible she had. More likely, though, Isabel had panicked over having an interview with Theo. Now, Hanna needed to find out why her mother would have gone to such lengths to avoid answering a cop's questions. Because that could mean Isabel had something to hide.

"We've had no visitor by that name," Dr. Warner said after she heard some computer clicks. "You think your mother might go to this woman?"

Hanna repeated her noncommittal sound. "Would it be possible for me to get a copy of my mother's visitors' log? She did give permission for you to discuss her medical records with me." At the time, Hanna hadn't wanted such access. It might come in handy now though. "I think my mother might have gotten a visitor who upset her. I'd like to know who."

She hoped lightning didn't strike her for that lie. Well, maybe it wasn't a lie. Such a visitor might exist, but Hanna wanted to look at the list to see if it was possible that Marlene had indeed paid a visit to Isabel and that she'd used an alias when she'd done that. Of course, Hanna might not recognize an alias. Might not recognize the names of any of her mother's visitors, but this was a start, and if she saw something suspicious, Jesse could no doubt run background checks to figure out if there was any connection to everything else that was going on.

"I'll email the visitors' list to you," the doctor confirmed. "And please let me know the moment you hear from your mother."

Hanna assured him that she would do just that, and then she tried to call Isabel. It didn't surprise her when it went straight to voice mail, but it added another layer of worry. Worry that Isabel wasn't just dodging everyone but had maybe been in an accident. Hanna left a message for Isabel to call her back right away.

She waited for Jesse to finish his conversation with Theo, and he looked as frustrated with this turn of events as she was. "This could be my fault," Hanna blurted out.

Jesse's forehead bunched up, but he looked skeptical about that. "How?" That sounded skeptical, too.

"I explained to you that I lied to my mother and told her that my memory was coming back. A couple of days later, Bull escaped from prison and someone kidnapped Marlene."

"Or Marlene faked her kidnapping," Jesse reminded her after he took a moment to process what she was trying to tell him. He huffed and put his hands on his hips while he stared at her. "You can't believe that, when Isabel told Marlene you might be getting your memory back, it prompted Marlene to convince her brother to escape so he could eliminate you before you remembered anything about your attack."

She shook her head. Hanna wasn't so sure she could believe that at all. "But maybe what happened was my mother was worried about Bull coming after me again if he got out of jail. Isabel maybe said or did something that led Bull to believe someone had ordered a hit on him. That could have been the reason he escaped."

After she heard her own words, she realized that sounded just as far-fetched as what Jesse had just tossed out there. The bottom line was she simply couldn't see her mother doing any of that.

But maybe that was because she didn't *want* to see it.

It could be she had on blinders when it came to Isabel. Her mother and she didn't have a stellar relationship and Hanna didn't have memories of Isabel raising her, but the woman was still her mother. It was hard to believe the worst about her, and this could most definitely fall into the worst category if it turned out Isabel was behind everything that had happened.

"Theo's going to get a warrant to take a look at Isabel's financials," Jesse told her. "It's routine for something like this since we'll have to investigate Marlene's accusation. Of course, after Grayson talks to Marlene, he'll also want to interview Isabel right away to get her side of the story."

Yes, interview her to either rule her out as a suspect. Or arrest her. But for that to happen, they had to find her first.

"It's time for me to go," Jesse said on a huff, and he went ahead into the nursery to see Evan.

As usual, the baby gave Jesse a big gummy grin and went right to him for a cuddle and kiss. But then Evan reached back for his grandmother who had now pulled out a stash of toys to go along with the books.

"I can watch him as long as you like," Melissa offered, obviously noting their troubled expressions.

"Thanks," Hanna told her. She just might need a little time to herself to tamp down the worry enough so that Evan didn't pick up on it. If the tamping down was even possible, that is. "Jesse's about to leave, and I'll be in the kitchen fixing Evan some lunch."

Hanna followed Jesse out of the nursery and, after she closed the door, he turned to her, their gazes locking. "I'll be okay," he said.

For a moment, she thought he was about to kiss her. For a moment, she thought she might *want* him to kiss her, too. But then his phone rang.

He muttered some profanity when Unknown Caller was on the screen. "Bull," he grumbled, and he put the call on speaker.

"You found my sister," Bull snarled like an accusation. "Where has she been? Who took her? Is she all right?"

"How'd you know Marlene had been found?" Jesse countered.

Bull wasn't so quick to jump with a response this time. "Police scanner," he finally said. "Is she all right?" he repeated, and this time his voice was much lower. Not calmer though. Either Bull was genuinely concerned about his sister or he was putting on a good act.

"She was conscious when she arrived here, but she does have a head injury," Jesse told him. "I'll give you more details about her at the meeting when you turn yourself in."

Bull stayed quiet for a moment. "Have you arrested my sister?"

Jesse paused, too. "Why would you ask that? Has Marlene done something to warrant an arrest?"

Bull cursed a spate of raw profanity. "Don't play games with me. Tell me if she has been or will be arrested."

"We can talk about that after you surrender," Jesse countered.

"No," Bull snapped after another long pause. "I'm not turning myself in. The meeting is off."

Jesse didn't get a chance to bargain with the man because Bull ended the call.

"Hell," Jesse snarled and immediately texted Grayson to let him know what Bull had said.

Hanna figured there were a lot of angry lawmen right now since they'd spent so much time and manpower to set this all up. But it was puzzling why Bull had pulled the plug on this when he hadn't gotten the answers he'd seemingly wanted about his sister. Of course, maybe that was an act and he had never intended to go through with turning himself in.

"I need to talk to Noah," Jesse muttered after he finished talking with Grayson and made the call to his cousin. "Bull backed out of the meeting," he told Noah, "but he knows his sister has resurfaced. He might try to come to the hospital."

"I'll be on the lookout for him," Noah assured him. "The hospital security guard is here with me, too."

"Good. Grayson will be there in about a half hour. How's Marlene?"

"Agitated and still demanding to speak to Hanna." Noah sighed, and in the background, Hanna could indeed hear the woman insisting on talking to her. "They've run some initial tests on her, and the nurse is cleaning and stitching up the head wound."

"Hanna," Marlene yelled again.

"Could you put her on the phone?" Hanna suggested. "Or should that wait until after she's interviewed?"

"Put Marlene on the phone," Jesse said after he gave it some thought.

Hanna heard some shuffling around and a few seconds later, Marlene spoke. "Hanna?"

"It's me," she verified. "What do you need to tell me?"

Marlene's breath hitched, and Hanna was pretty sure the woman was crying. "I can't tell you over the phone. I have to see you, please," she begged. "Because I know the reason you were shot."

Chapter Nine

"This is the right thing to do," Jesse heard Hanna murmur. Not for the first time either. She'd already said a variation of that while Jesse had been making the security arrangements for Marlene to be brought to Hanna's.

Arrangements he sure as hell hadn't wanted to make.

He'd much rather keep Marlene as far away as possible so that Hanna and Evan would be safe. Well, as safe as he could make them anyway. With Bull still at large, Isabel missing, and perhaps a rogue ATF agent on their hands, maybe no place was truly free from danger. But as Hanna had pointed out, they were the likely targets. Perhaps Marlene, too. So, for that reason, it was best to go ahead and meet with the woman and hear what she had to say.

Of course, while Marlene had still been on the phone, Jesse had pressed the woman to clarify the reason she'd said what she had.

Because I know the reason you were shot.

But Marlene had continued to insist that she would

only tell Hanna face-to-face. Part of Jesse wanted to dig in his heels and flat-out refuse. The other part of him wanted to hear what she had to say. Since Hanna was in the camp of wanting to hear out Marlene, too, he'd finally given in and made arrangements for an EMT to bring Marlene to Hanna's. That wasn't ideal, but it was much better than having Hanna leave the house and make the drive to the hospital. A trip like that would have meant traveling on a road where a shooter could easily be lying in wait for them. Especially if that shooter was working with Marlene and knew when to expect them to come driving along.

Even with having the meeting at Hanna's house, it had still taken time and coordination to put all the pieces in place for the visit. First, Marlene had had to get her doctor on board with the idea. According to the doctor, her injuries weren't that serious, but he'd wanted to keep her in the hospital for observation for at least twenty-four hours because of her concussion. Marlene had likely pressured him to agree to the plan by promising to return to the hospital as soon as she'd had her chat with Hanna.

Jesse had arranged for two deputies to accompany the EMTs and Marlene just in case Marlene turned out to be a target. Then he'd beefed up security at Hanna's by asking Deputy Ava Lawson to stay with Melissa and Evan in the nursery while the ranch hands and a reserve deputy kept watch of the grounds. They could still be attacked, but Jesse had made it as secure as he possibly could.

Now, Marlene had better come through on the

promise of this revelation as to the reason Hanna had been shot. If not, Jesse intended to charge the woman with obstruction of justice and withholding evidence. He had zero tolerance for someone who could put Hanna and Evan at risk.

Hanna was pacing her living room while she kept her attention nailed to the baby monitor. Jesse had taken a look at it, too, and knew that Evan was having a blast with his grandmother and the deputy entertaining him. The plan, though, was for that entertainment to not have to go on too long. He knew that Hanna would breathe easier once they had Marlene in and out of the house and she could then be with their son.

Jesse silently groaned when his phone rang and, for a moment, he thought it might be Marlene canceling. But no. It was Agent Shaw. Since he didn't want the distraction, Jesse considered not answering it, but then he remembered that Bull had known about Marlene surfacing, and it was possible he'd gotten that info from the agent. If Shaw was in contact with Bull, then it was something Jesse needed to know.

"Make it quick," Jesse snarled when he answered.

"I want to be there when Marlene is questioned," Shaw immediately insisted.

Shaw would have obviously known they would interview the woman. Had to, since she was either the victim of a serious crime or she wanted law enforcement to believe that she was.

"This is my investigation too," Shaw went on, obviously taking Jesse's silence as a no. "I should at least be allowed to observe in case she describes or mentions someone in the militia. I've studied the files of every known member, and I might be able to help ID the person who either kidnapped her or assisted her in this plan."

"If Marlene's behind her own kidnapping, she isn't likely to give us an accurate description of anyone who helped her," Jesse pointed out, his voice a growl. "But you can request to see a recording of the interview whenever it happens."

"What do you mean *whenever*?" Shaw snapped back. "Marlene was taken from the hospital, and it's obvious she's on the way to speak to Hanna and you."

Jesse didn't bother to groan. Nor did it surprise him that the agent had the hospital under surveillance.

"I'm not interviewing Marlene," Jesse told him. "Not officially." Though he would Mirandize her in case she spilled something that incriminated her or someone else.

"It doesn't have to be official for me to need to know what she says," Shaw argued. "I need to be there."

This time Jesse voiced that no. "That's not going to happen." He couldn't risk having two of his suspects in the house, especially since they could be working together. "Like I said, contact the sheriff and work out your part, or lack thereof, in the official interview. I have to go."

He ended the call before Shaw could continue to press, but Jesse knew that wasn't the last he'd hear from the man. Nope. Shaw would likely just show up here, and that's why Jesse sent a text to the deputy patrolling the grounds to tell him not to let Shaw near the house. The ATF might give him and the sheriff's office some flak about that, but Jesse was in the "better safe than sorry" mode.

"Agent Shaw's coming here?" Hanna asked, the concern coming through loud and clear in her voice and expression.

"No," Jesse assured her, and even though it was probably a bad idea and a distraction, he went to her and pulled her into his arms.

She didn't resist. In fact, Hanna was the one who moved closer. "I just need this to be over," she muttered.

Yeah, he was on that very same page, and the stress and worry were eating away at both of them. Jesse brushed what he hoped would be a kiss of comfort on her forehead, but as he did that, Hanna looked up. Their eyes met. Held.

And, man, did he feel that gut punch of heat.

It was the kind of heat that made him remember just how strong this attraction had been and still was between them. It also made him forget that the timing for it sucked. So did the timing for the kiss. But that didn't stop Jesse from lowering his head and touching his mouth to hers.

He got an even hotter jolt of heat. A jolt that shot through every inch of him when Hanna moved right into the kiss. When she turned it from something comforting to scorching.

The chain he'd kept on this heat snapped and Jesse dragged her closer to him. Until they were mouth to

mouth. Body to body. Hanna certainly wasn't resist-
ing, and he could feel the hunger. The need. Things
that had always been there between them. Her mouth
moved over his as if there'd been no breakup, no
shooting. As if it were just the two of them ready to
haul each other off to bed.

That couldn't happen, of course.

Jesse mentally repeated that to himself and kept
repeating it until he got this fierce need back on the
leash. Until he could finally end the sweet torture of
her mouth and taste.

"I'm sorry," she immediately breathed.

He didn't bother telling her that an apology wasn't
necessary. Or wanted. Jesse just pushed the limits of
his willpower a little bit longer by brushing a kiss
on her mouth. A kiss to remind her that an apology
wasn't going to cool the fire. And that he fully intended to do this again, and more, the first chance
they got.

She nodded as if she understood his point, and
she continued to look up at him. Her eyes were wide,
her face was flushed, and she was breathing through
her mouth. All signs that made him wish taking her
to bed was an actual option. Right now, no waiting.

But he quickly got a reminder of why that couldn't
happen.

At the sound of the approaching vehicles, Hanna
practically jerked away from him, and she pulled back
her shoulders. Bracing herself. Jesse steeled himself
up in a different kind of way. He put his hand over
his weapon while he checked the window and spot-

ted the Silver Creek cruiser. He continued to keep his hand on his gun after he opened the door. Even though Marlene was under heavy guard, it would be the ideal time for someone to launch an attack.

The EMT who accompanied Marlene stayed in the cruiser, but with Grayson on one side of her and Theo on the other, they led Marlene toward the house. There was now a bandage on the woman's head, and she was wearing a pair of green scrubs. Probably because her own clothes had already been bagged and sent to the lab for processing.

Grayson and Theo moved fast to get Marlene inside, Grayson scowling when a car came to a quick stop behind the cruiser. "Agent Shaw," he grumbled. "I'll handle this."

Jesse was glad Grayson had offered to do that since he didn't want to take his attention off Marlene. Added to that, Shaw could be there to launch that attack they were all worried about, so he had to be questioned. Had to be contained if he tried to get into the house.

Theo led Marlene inside, and Grayson went off to confront the agent. Jesse was thankful for it, too, since he wanted to focus on Marlene.

Marlene, however, obviously had her focus on Hanna. "Thank you for seeing me," Marlene said. She was trembling a little, and her voice was shaky.

Hanna nodded, but she didn't press the woman to jump right into an explanation of why she'd said what she had. *I know the reason you were shot.* But

Loyal Readers
FREE BOOKS Voucher

We're giving away **THOUSANDS** of **FREE BOOKS**

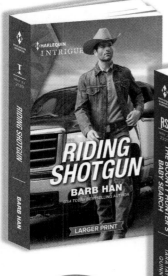

Get up to 4 FREE FABULOUS BOOKS You Love!

To thank you for being a loyal reader we'd like to send you up to 4 FREE BOOKS, absolutely free when you try the Harlequin Reader Service.

Just write "YES" on the Loyal Reader Voucher and we'll send you 2 free books from each series you choose and a Free Mystery Gift, altogether worth over $20.

Try **Harlequin® Romantic Suspense** and get 2 books featuring heart-racing page-turners with unexpected plot twists and irresistible chemistry that will keep you guessing to the very end.

Try **Harlequin Intrigue® Larger-Print** and get 2 books featuring action-packed stories that will keep you on the edge of your seat. Solve the crime and deliver justice at all costs

Or TRY BOTH and get 2 books from each series!

Your free books are completely free, even the shipping! If you continue with your subscription, you can look forward to curated monthly shipments of brand-new books from your selected series, always at a discount off the cover price! Plus you can cancel any time.

So don't miss out, return your Loyal Readers Voucher today to get your Free books.

Pam Powers

LOYAL READER
FREE BOOKS VOUCHER

Marlene thankfully didn't waste any time. The fewer minutes she was in the house, the better.

"You'll want to know what happened to me," Marlene volunteered, looking at Jesse now. "I've already told Grayson and Theo, but you'll need to hear it, too."

Despite Jesse wanting to hear what she had to say, he held up his hand to put the pause button on this. "Have you been read your rights?" he asked.

Marlene nodded. "Grayson did that. He said it was routine."

Jesse got a confirming nod from Theo before he motioned for Marlene to continue.

"You'll need to help Grayson and Theo to make sure I'm not taken again." She stopped, blinked back tears. "Oh, God. They want me dead."

"*They*?" Jesse questioned, not reacting to the woman's crying. And he wouldn't. Not until he was convinced he could trust her, and they were a long way from that happening.

"The militia. My brother," Marlene revealed. Since her trembling got worse, Theo helped her to the sofa and had her sit.

"You think Bull had you kidnapped?" Jesse pressed. Neither Hanna nor he sat. They stood side by side, looking down at the woman. "And what does your kidnapping have to do with what you insist you have to tell Hanna?"

"It might have everything to do with it," Marlene muttered, and she swiped away a tear that slid down her cheek. "Let me start from the beginning. Well, one beginning anyway. Years ago, I had a relationship with Arnie Ross."

Jesse was sure he blinked. Of all the possibilities he'd considered of what the woman might say, that one hadn't been on his radar.

"I know, Arnie doesn't look like my type." Marlene shook her head. "But this was before he started using drugs. Your mother can tell you just how handsome and charming Arnie used to be," she added.

It took Jesse a moment to realize that Marlene had aimed that comment at Hanna. "Isabel knew Arnie?" Jesse asked.

"Yes," Marlene confirmed. "She dated him when they were in college. I figured she'd told you."

"Maybe," Hanna admitted in a whisper, and her forehead creased with fresh worry.

Perhaps Isabel had told her before Hanna had lost her memory, but if so, that made Jesse wonder why the heck Isabel hadn't mentioned it after the shooting. He hoped Isabel had a good explanation. Of course, first they'd have to find the woman to get any answers.

"Charming and handsome," Marlene repeated. "But that was all before he got involved with the militia. An involvement I figure he used to feed his addiction since he'd already blown through his inheritance and trust fund by then."

"Any reason you didn't tell us about all of this when we were investigating Hanna's and Arnie's shootings?" Jesse didn't bother to take the anger out of his voice. Marlene shouldn't have withheld any info whether or not she thought it was pertinent.

"Because I didn't want anyone to know I'd had a relationship with a man like that. My business associates wouldn't understand." Marlene locked gazes with him. "And I swear I didn't have anything to do with the militia. I didn't even know Arnie was involved in that until hours before he was killed."

That got Jesse's full attention. "How did you find out?"

Marlene swallowed hard. "I'd dropped by to see Bull. He wasn't in his house, he was on his back porch. I overheard him talking to Arnie on the phone about a shipment of guns coming in. I can't recall Bull's exact words, but I could tell it was something illegal, and he mentioned the Brotherhood. I knew that's what the militia members called it."

Jesse had plenty of questions for Marlene, including how all of this connected to Hanna, but he went with a simple one. "You're sure your brother was talking to Arnie?"

"Yes," she quickly confirmed. "He said Arnie's name a couple of times, and it sounded as if Bull was angry with him. Lecturing him, you know, like demanding that Arnie stay sober until the shipment was done."

Hanna and Jesse exchanged a glance, and he saw some of the same skepticism in her eyes that he was also feeling. If Bull truly was a deep cover ATF agent, then why the heck would he have had that level of trust with a known drug user? Shaw might have some insight on that, but even if Shaw was clean, he would only know the info Bull had given him. Info that might be a bunch of lies.

"If I hadn't overheard that conversation," Marlene went on, shifting her attention to Hanna, "you might have never been shot."

Hanna didn't make a sound, but Jesse could practically feel the muscles in her body turn to steel. "What do you mean?" Hanna asked.

More tears welled in Marlene's eyes and she gathered her breath. "I confronted Bull. I demanded to know what he was involved with. He blew me off, saying I misheard him, that he wasn't involved with the militia. I played along because I didn't want him to know I was suspicious, and on the way back home, I stopped by Arnie's."

Jesse's skepticism went up a notch. "You went alone to visit a drug user you suspected was a member of a dangerous militia group?"

"I know it was a stupid thing to do," Marlene blurted out, "but I was worried about my brother. I just wanted to talk with Arnie and try to get him to admit if Bull was involved in something that would get him hurt. Or killed." She drew in another long breath. "I tried to keep the conversation casual, and I didn't specifically ask anything about the call I overheard or the militia, but Arnie figured out why I was really there."

"What did he do?" Jesse prompted when the woman didn't continue.

Marlene cleared her throat. "He was angry. Furious. And he said I should keep my mouth shut if I didn't want to have to visit my brother behind bars. I managed to get him calmed down. At least, I thought I had. I swore I wouldn't tell anyone, and I left." Her voice hitched and she pressed her trembling fingers to her mouth for a moment. "But he must not have been calm at all because that night he went to the ranch to confront you. That night, he shot Hanna."

Jesse thought about that for a couple of seconds and couldn't totally dismiss that the conversation with Marlene had played a small part in spurring Arnie to come to the ranch. But Jesse was betting it was the news of the man's imminent arrest that had sent Arnie on the fateful trip.

And that was right back on Jesse.

Jesse would have liked to put some of the blame for the shooting onto Marlene, but he couldn't. Arnie and Bull had come to the ranch because Jesse hadn't been fast enough in making that arrest. It didn't matter that he'd still been trying to build a case against the men. He should have moved sooner, should have had them behind bars so they couldn't hurt Hanna or anyone else.

"Are you convinced that Bull was trying to stop Arnie from shooting Hanna, or do you believe he was responsible for it happening?" Jesse asked bluntly.

Marlene certainly didn't voice a quick answer this time. "I don't think my brother is innocent," she finally said. "In fact, I think he's the one who arranged to have me kidnapped."

All right then. Maybe they were getting somewhere. Then again, the only place they might be getting with this was where Marlene was trying to lead them.

"Why would you say that?" Jesse asked, hopeful that the woman had some actual proof and not just suspicions. "Did you actually see Bull when you were taken? Because earlier, you thought Isabel was the one who'd arranged your kidnapping."

"No, I didn't see him or Isabel," she said on a heavy sigh. "And Isabel might have had a part in it. I can't be sure."

Jesse huffed. "What are you sure of then?"

"Like I told Grayson and Theo, I heard someone on the back porch of my house. I thought it was a stray dog who'd been coming to the door, but when I opened it, a man wearing a ski mask hit me on the head." She lightly touched the bandage. "He knocked me out and apparently drugged me, too. The next thing I remember, I woke up blindfolded and tied to a chair."

"Where?" Jesse immediately asked.

"A cabin."

Jesse looked at Theo to get his take on that. "She was able to give us a description of the place where she was held, and the CSIs are heading out there to take a look. We believe it could be one of the old fishing cabins on the north fork of Silver Creek."

Good. Maybe the CSIs would find something to shed some light on all of this.

"Did your kidnapper speak or tell you why you'd been taken?" Jesse continued.

"Oh, he spoke, all right," Marlene verified with some anger in her tone now. "It wasn't Bull, but the man threatened to kill me if I didn't give him my ATM card and pin and the location and combination of the safe at my house."

So, the motive was money. Well, maybe. Jesse was still deciding whether or not Marlene was giving them the full story.

"The safe had been emptied," Theo confirmed. "But the ATM card wasn't used."

"I had ten thousand in cash in the safe," Marlene explained. "And some family jewelry. Theo said my attacker took that, too."

"Did he bring the money and jewelry to the cabin?" Jesse wanted to know.

"No. After I told him about the safe and gave him my ATM card, he left and didn't come back. Other than that glimpse of him before he hit me, I didn't see him, but Bull must have sent him to get the money from me. He must have been part of the militia."

That would certainly fit, but Jesse recalled how upset Bull had seemed when he'd learned his sister had been taken. Of course, Bull could have faked that. Or maybe it was Bull's plan and he hadn't intended for Marlene to be hurt.

"How'd you escape?" Jesse prodded.

Marlene held up her wrist for him to see the bandages there. There were also abrasions around her ankles. "I just kept tugging and pulling until I got free. Then I got out of the cabin and started running."

"Marlene said she ran to the nearest cabin, but no

one was there." Theo filled him in when the woman stopped. "But there was the old car, and the key was under the mat. She used the car to come here to Hanna's."

"Why not go to the sheriff's office?" Jesse queried.

Marlene shook her head. "I wasn't thinking straight, and Hanna's house was on the way."

Depending on which road Marlene had taken, Hanna's could have indeed been on the way, but the most common instinct should have been for Marlene to go straight to the cops. Still, it was possible she had been drugged, so that could have played into her decision.

"We still haven't found Marlene's car," Theo disclosed, "and we're processing the truck left at her house."

"The truck the kidnapper must have used," Marlene provided. "He put me in my car and drove to the cabin."

"We told her that Bull had been spotted earlier in a truck that matches that description," Theo told Jesse.

"And that's another reason why I believe my brother has to be involved. First, the militia connection and now the truck," Marlene muttered, and she got to her feet. "I don't want to think he would do something like this, but I can't just bury my head in the sand. I've told Grayson and Theo this, and I'm telling you now. If Bull contacts me, I'll let you know ASAP. He has to be stopped."

If he was behind all of this, then yes, he would be

stopped, and if Marlene could help with that, then something good had come out of this chat.

"Have you remembered anything about the shooting?" Marlene asked, turning to face Hanna. "Did Arnie say anything about me being the reason he hurried to the ranch to confront Jesse?" She made a hoarse sob. "I hope and pray I wasn't the reason."

Hanna stared at her a couple of seconds and shook her head. "I'm sorry, but I still don't have any memories of that night."

Marlene nodded, wiped away some tears and headed for the door.

"Grayson will be doing the official interview as soon as we get her back to the hospital," Theo murmured to him. "I'll let you know if we get anything new from that."

Jesse followed them to the door and saw Grayson on the phone while he waited by the cruiser. There was no sign of Shaw. Good. Jesse hadn't wanted him hanging around. However, he knew they hadn't seen the last of the agent.

The moment Theo and Grayson had Marlene back in the cruiser, Jesse went ahead and shut the door and locked up. He was thankful they had the room to themselves, not because he had plans to kiss her again, but because he wanted her take on everything Marlene had just told them.

"First chance I get, I'll be asking my mother about Arnie," she insisted. "I was telling Marlene the truth when I said my mother hasn't mentioned that since the shooting." She paused. "But, of course, I am getting back some of my memory."

Jesse studied her eyes. "Memories about the shooting?"

She shook her head. "About us." Hanna made a vague motion toward the hall and the bedrooms. "When you kissed me, I got flashes of when we were together."

Together as in when they'd had sex. "I hope they were good flashes," he said, trying to keep it light.

Her mouth quivered a little. Not in a bad way. But it was as if she was fighting a smile. "Good ones," she verified.

That might have sent him right to her for another of those ill-advised kisses, but the sound of his phone ringing shot through the room. Jesse frowned when he saw the call was from the ranch hand, Miguel Navarro. Hell. He hoped Agent Shaw hadn't returned.

"A problem?" Jesse immediately asked when he answered.

"Yeah, a big one," Miguel confirmed. "I spotted an armed man in a ski mask. He ducked into some trees, but I think he was heading straight for the house."

Chapter Ten

Even though Jesse hadn't put the call on speaker, Hanna had no trouble hearing what the ranch hand had just told him.

There was a gunman coming to the house.

Oh, mercy. If that person shot at them, Evan could be hit.

"Go to the nursery," Jesse insisted. "Lock the door and tell Deputy Lawson to stand guard."

Hanna desperately wanted to get to her son, but she was also concerned about Jesse. "What will you do?"

"I'll stop whoever it is from getting to Evan or you."

He was all cop now, and Hanna knew he was good at his job, but that wouldn't stop her from worrying that he could be hurt. Or worse.

"Be careful," she cautioned. Hanna held his gaze a moment longer before he went to the window and she hurried to the nursery.

"One of the hands spotted a gunman," Hanna explained to the deputy and Jesse's mom when she rushed in.

The alarm fired through Melissa's eyes. She was

in the rocking chair, holding Evan, who was obviously getting a head start on his afternoon nap. The tray with the baby's lunch was on the table, his empty bottle sitting next to it.

Whipping out her phone, Ava locked the door. "Best if the three of you get into the bathroom," the deputy advised, making a call while she raced to the window.

Hanna yanked out a quilt that she kept folded by the crib, and she went into the bathroom to put it in the tub. She forced herself not to give in to the fear. Not to be terrified for Jesse, for all of them. That wouldn't help, and right now she had to take some steps to make sure Evan was as safe as he could be.

Even though Melissa's heart had to be beating hard and fast, she managed to get into the tub with Evan without waking him up. Hopefully, he'd stay asleep, and while she was hoping, Hanna added that maybe one of the people guarding the house would catch the gunman before he could do any damage.

"Stay down," Ava called out to them. "An armed man was just spotted in the backyard."

Hanna couldn't hold back the slam of fear this time. Was this a second attacker? Or had the other one gone back there? Since they were likely dealing with a militia, it was possible they had sent several men.

But why?

That was the question that continued to race through her head. Was she the target? If so, was it because of something she might remember?

Groaning, she sank down into the tub across from Melissa and the baby, and she tried to will the memories to come. It didn't work. It was as if her brain had gone on lockdown and a wave of pure frustration coated the fear and worry.

The sound of a shot cracked through the air. Along with causing her heart to pound against her chest, it caused Hanna to latch onto Melissa so she could pull her lower in the tub. The woman ended up on her back with Evan nestled in her arm. There wasn't enough room for Hanna to lie down next to them, but she stayed as low as she could and prayed that bullet hadn't hit anyone but the intruder.

There was another gunshot blast. Then another. The sound whipped up Hanna's adrenaline and vised her lungs so that it was hard for her to breathe. Unfortunately, it didn't shut down the horrible thoughts she was having about Jesse. He was probably out there. Probably right in the line of fire, and he was doing that not only because it was his job but because he would protect them.

"It'll be okay," Melissa whispered, and Hanna heard the woman mutter a prayer. This had to be terrifying for her, too, since that was her son out there.

Hanna's phone dinged with a text. Her hands were shaking when she pulled it from her pocket and saw Jesse's name on the screen. Thank God, he was alive.

Isabel just pulled into the driveway. We're getting someone to her now.

Sweet heaven. Now her mother was out there in harm's way. But Hanna had to immediately rethink that. Was it actually harm's way or was this part of some plan to silence her before her memory could return? She didn't want to think the worst about her mother, but someone was behind this, and Isabel hadn't exactly been forthcoming about knowing Arnie.

She showed Melissa the text so that she'd know Jesse hadn't been hurt, and the woman's face relaxed just a little. "You know, I was a deputy when Grayson arrested your father."

Hanna shook her head. She hadn't known that, but of course, the timing worked since that arrest would have happened about thirty years ago.

"Your mother was so angry, and she attacked Grayson," Melissa went on. "She scratched his face and tried to stab him with a letter opener."

Even with everything else going on outside, that shocked Hanna. "Did Grayson arrest her?"

"No, he said it was just a fit of anger and that she had enough to deal with. He didn't want both your parents in jail, I guess."

Again, the timing for this wasn't stellar, but Hanna asked the question anyway. "Was my father guilty? Did he assault the young woman?"

"He never confessed, but all the evidence pointed to him, and there was an eyewitness. Mason," she supplied.

Hanna groaned. Isabel wouldn't have cared much

for that, and it added another layer of her hatred for the Rylands.

"You should just be careful around Isabel," Melissa suggested. "I don't like to stir up trouble, but she wants to put a wedge between Jesse and you." She paused. "After Evan was born and you were still in the hospital, Isabel even threatened to try to get custody of Evan."

Another blow. Good grief. Just what lengths would Isabel go because of this old feud between the Rylands and her?

"Was I wrong to tell you all of that?" Melissa asked. She winced, shook her head. "Of course, I was wrong. Let's just say I no longer have nerves of steel the way I did when I wore a badge."

"You weren't wrong to tell me," Hanna assured her, and the woman's nerves seemed just fine to her.

"Stay put, but they've got the two men," Ava called out to them.

The relief came, but it was just as much of a punch as the adrenaline. And the worry was still there. "Is everyone okay?" Hanna asked the deputy, and she could have sworn her heart skipped a couple of beats when Ava didn't immediately answer.

"One of the gunmen is dead," Ava relayed, coming to the bathroom door. She still had her gun gripped in her hand. "No one else was hurt. Jesse and Grayson have the second man."

More relief came because Jesse and the others were okay. Better yet, they had someone in custody. "Who is it?" Hanna wanted to know.

"Not sure yet, but it wasn't any of our persons of interest."

So, not Shaw, and Hanna had known it wasn't Marlene or her mother because it was a man. However, that didn't mean one of the two women hadn't hired someone to do this.

The seconds crawled by while they waited, and Hanna tried to keep herself steady by watching the peaceful, rhythmic rise and fall of Evan's breathing. Unfortunately, it didn't cause much peace inside her because she couldn't stop thinking about those two men, and the person who'd hired them, putting her precious little boy in jeopardy.

"It's Jesse," Ava announced when she got a text. She went to the nursery door where Hanna heard her unlock it.

A moment later, Jesse walked in, and Hanna couldn't stop herself. She got out of the tub, hurried to him and clamped her arms around him. All the steeling up she'd done nearly vanished thanks to the relief at seeing he truly was unharmed.

"You're okay," Hanna murmured.

He nodded, ran his hand down the length of her hair and shifted his attention to his mom and Evan. "You can come back into the nursery now," he assured them, and they both helped Melissa out of the tub. "I locked up the house and reset the security. Ava will be staying inside with us until Grayson is sure the scene is secure."

That didn't help with the nerves. Someone else could be out there. But by now, Grayson probably had every available deputy either on scene or on the way.

When they were back in the nursery, Melissa immediately returned to the rocking chair. Maybe because, like Hanna, her legs were a little shaky. The rocking would also help to keep Evan asleep.

"Who are the gunmen?" Hanna asked him in a whisper so they wouldn't wake the baby.

Jesse shook his head. "I don't know either of them, and neither had any ID. Grayson will be taking the live one in for questioning, so we might know something soon."

"Maybe he'll want a deal and will give up the name of the person who sent him." She paused. "Someone did send them, right?"

"It looks that way. If they'd been local with a grudge against me, or you, I would have recognized them. Grayson can compare their photos to those of yet-to-be-identified militia members. We might get a match. Might get a match, too, when we run their prints."

Yes, because men like that probably had criminal records.

"I heard gunshots," Hanna said. "You're sure no one other than the gunman was hit?"

"Positive. The dead gunman fired two of the shots." He stopped, muttered some profanity, and she saw that was eating away at him as much as it was her. Those shots could have gone through the walls. "Grayson fired the third shot and killed him. The second man surrendered. Well, he surrendered after Grayson, me and the ranch hands all had our weapons pointed at him."

Jesse kept staring at her. "Did the sound of the shots trigger…anything for you?"

He was asking if she was on the verge of a panic attack. She wasn't, so Hanna shook her head. But she was well past the stage of being riled to the core.

"Where's my mother?" she asked.

"In her car with a ranch hand standing guard to make sure she stays put. She wants to see you, of course."

"Of course," Hanna mumbled. "I'll want to see her, too, and demand to know if she had any part in this."

Jesse did another of those soothing hand strokes, this time down her arm. "Trust me, I want to know the same thing." He hesitated a heartbeat. "Agent Shaw is out there, too."

Hanna groaned. "Why is he here? Did he have something to do with the gunmen?"

"He claims he just wanted to ask about what Marlene had told us," Jesse answered.

"You believe him?" she asked.

"Right now, I'm not inclined to believe him, Marlene, or your mother."

"I agree," Hanna couldn't say fast enough.

Jesse's phone dinged with a text, and he frowned when he read the message. "Grayson said your mother's been searched. She's not armed, and he wants to know if you want her to come inside for that chat?"

Hanna didn't have to debate that answer either. "Yes. Let's go ahead and get this over with."

She wanted to do this while the adrenaline was still high, while she still had very vivid feelings of how close her son and Jesse could have come to being hurt today. Two shots. That's how many bullets Jesse said the gunman had fired.

Two shots that could have been deadly to anyone in the vicinity.

"If you don't mind, I'll just keep holding Evan instead of putting him in his crib," Melissa told them.

"Please do," Hanna agreed. "I'll come and get him when I finish talking to my mother."

"Good luck," Melissa whispered to her and, considering the conversation they'd just had, Jesse's mom no doubt knew this was not going to be a pleasant mother-daughter kind of chat.

Ava stayed put with Melissa while Jesse and she went to the front of the house. Jesse disengaged the security, unlocked the door and motioned to someone. Grayson, probably, because several moments later Isabel and he stepped onto the porch. Isabel actually froze, probably because she noted the expression on Hanna's face, but then she broke into a run and pulled Hanna into her arms.

"You're okay. Thank God, you're okay," Isabel said, her words rushing out. "I need to see Evan just to make sure he's all right, too."

"He's sleeping, and I don't want him disturbed." Hanna could hear the cold edge in her voice and didn't have plans to warm it up any time soon.

Isabel must have sensed the iciness, as well, because she let go of Hanna and backed up a few steps while she studied her face. Behind Isabel, Jesse went through the routine of locking up again—something

Hanna was thankful for since she didn't want any other hired guns using this visit as a ploy to launch another attack.

"What's wrong?" Isabel asked.

Hanna nearly laughed. "You mean other than the obvious? Two gunmen came to my home, probably to try to kill Jesse or me, and one of them fired shots that could have hit Evan." Her voice had gotten louder with each word until Hanna nearly shouted the last part.

Isabel frantically shook her head. "You're acting as if I had something to do with that. I didn't." And she aimed a scalding glare at Jesse when he went to Hanna's side. "You're responsible for this—"

"Hush and answer some questions," Hanna said. She didn't shout this time, but she returned the glare that her mother had aimed at Jesse.

That caused Isabel's shoulders to snap back. "What is it you think I've done?"

"Oh, where to start," Hanna grumbled. "How about you explain why you just left the rehab facility without telling anyone? And why you haven't answered your phone. And while you're at it, explain why you did that when you should have been giving a Silver Creek deputy a statement about the investigation that could have prevented the shooting here today."

All right, so she hadn't totally gotten her voice under control; Hanna could hear the hard snarl in her tone. But it must have worked because Isabel didn't launch into more glaring and didn't aim any accusations at Jesse.

"I panicked," Isabel finally said, and she looked both disgusted with herself and ashamed. "I thought Deputy Ryland was there at the facility because I was a suspect in your attack. I had nothing to do with that," she stressed.

Hanna would put that last part on hold and stated the obvious. "If you're innocent, why run? Why not stay put, answer the deputy's questions, and clear your name?"

"Because he's a Ryland," Isabel railed. The venom had returned. "Maybe not in name, but he was raised by them. He's loyal to them. They've always had it in for me, and I wasn't going to sit there while Deputy Sheldon made false accusations."

Jesse lifted his hand as Hanna started to fire off another question, stunning Isabel by reciting the Miranda warning. That certainly didn't improve Isabel's mood, and she was spitting mad by the time he'd finished. But Hanna was glad he'd done it. If her mother did say something incriminating, she definitely wanted it used against her, to make sure she was punished for any wrongdoing.

"One of the things Deputy Sheldon intended to ask you about were some phone calls you got from Marlene. And before you say you didn't get them," Jesse added when Isabel opened her mouth, "you should know that we've seen the phone records and we know the calls were made."

Isabel closed her mouth and her jaw tightened.

Hanna was pretty sure she'd been about to lie. "So what if Marlene and I talked? I told you we're in the same social circles, and every now and then we talk about parties, events and such."

Jesse kept his lethal cop's stare on her.

"All right," Isabel admitted grudgingly. "And sometimes I vented to her about Hanna and you, about how I didn't want the two of you together."

"Why Marlene?" Jesse persisted. "Did you believe she could do something to make sure Hanna stayed away from me?"

"No," her mother blurted. "Of course not. Like I said, I was just venting."

"The timing of that venting is suspicious," Jesse pointed out, not easing up on his stare. "One long phone call the day before Hanna was shot and two more the day after. It seems odd to me that you'd be *venting* about Hanna and me being together when your daughter was in the hospital fighting for her life."

Isabel's breath was gusting now and on a loud groan, she turned and sank down onto the sofa. "I felt guilty because I'd told Marlene those things. I was scared I was going to lose my daughter and my grandson, and I needed someone to talk to."

"And you chose to call someone in your social circle rather than a friend," Jesse reminded her.

"I don't have many friends," Isabel admitted on a heavy sigh. "And Marlene lives in Silver Creek, so she knows my history with your family. Some of my acquaintances don't."

The woman stopped, stayed quiet a moment. When she lifted her gaze to meet Jesse's, it was obvious she had calmed down some. Not Hanna though. Nothing her mother had said cleared her of suspicion.

"Look, I didn't have anything to do with the shooting and I've got nothing to do with the militia," Isabel insisted. "And I don't know why you think I'm connected to any of this. Those phone calls have nothing to do with what's going on. This is just you trying to poison my daughter's mind so she'll go back to you. Well, that's not going to work—"

"Stop," Hanna said when the images and sounds started to fly through her head. Memories, maybe. Of her mother's face when she'd been angry like this. Maybe when Hanna had told her she was pregnant with Jesse's child?

No.

Not then. In the flash that Hanna got, she was already mega pregnant, so that was an argument they'd have had months earlier. This was something else. But it wasn't anything she could put her finger on.

"What is it?" Isabel slowly got to her feet. "Are you in pain? Did you—"

"Arnie and you used to be lovers," Hanna blurted out to stop her mother from asking more questions. "And you said something to him about Jesse and me."

The first part was true. Well, according to Marlene anyway. But the last part was a bluff, yet Hanna immediately saw that she'd hit the mark. The color blanched from Isabel's face and that's when Hanna realized it hadn't actually been a bluff after all. During that argument flashing through her head, she recalled her mother mentioning Arnie's name.

"Are you remembering...something?" Isabel asked. Still no color in her face and her voice was trembling.

"What did you say to Arnie about Jesse and me? And don't deny it," Hanna warned her. "I'm remembering enough to know if you're lying or not."

Isabel's throat worked when she swallowed. "I just thought Arnie could cause some trouble for Jesse, that's all."

That's all. Well, it didn't sound so innocent to Hanna, considering Arnie was a drug user and in the militia. And the flashes of memories weren't innocent either. She and her mother had had a full-fledged argument.

"What kind of trouble?" Hanna demanded, not taking her gaze off her mother.

"Nothing violent," Isabel rushed to say. She volleyed her attention between Jesse and her. "I swear, I didn't tell him to do anything violent. I sure as heck didn't tell him to drag my pregnant daughter out of her car and try to kill her."

Everything inside Hanna went still. And cold. An icy cold that went all the way to the bone.

"What did you tell him to do?" Hanna restated, enunciating each word through her now-clenched teeth.

Several moments crawled by before the woman spoke again. "I just warned him that if he didn't do something about Jesse that he was going to find himself in jail."

"When did you do that?" Jesse demanded. "When?" he snapped when Isabel turned away and started to cry.

"I told him that right before he went to the ranch and shot my daughter," Isabel muttered.

And with that confession, Isabel broke into a full sob.

Chapter Eleven

The adrenaline from the attack had come and gone, leaving Jesse with a fatigue that felt like he'd been drained dry. He was pretty sure Hanna was experiencing the same thing, but they were still doing what was necessary to take care of Evan while they waited for updates on the investigation.

Fortunately, the fatigue and stress didn't seem to be affecting Evan one bit. He was babbling and smiling while he ate his dinner in his high chair.

After Grayson had cleared the scene, Melissa and Ava had left, but the ranch hands and a reserve deputy stayed on the grounds to keep watch. Jesse hoped they wouldn't be necessary, that whoever was behind the attack wouldn't send someone else to try to finish the job, but he would keep the backup in place until he was sure it was safe.

Whenever the heck that would be.

At least they didn't have to deal with Isabel. After her tear-filled confession, she'd finally left with Grayson to give a statement on the info she'd withheld after Hanna's shooting. Info that Isabel kept insisting wasn't relevant, that it wasn't the reason Arnie had dragged Hanna out of her car.

But Jesse had heard the doubt in the woman's voice.

Had seen it on her face.

Despite what she was saying, Isabel did indeed blame herself. Of course, that particular layer of guilt might be just the tip of the iceberg because they still hadn't been able to rule her out as a suspect. He couldn't necessarily see her running a militia, but it was possible she was somehow involved with it. The fact that she'd had contact with Arnie at the time of Hanna's shooting proved that Isabel had stayed in touch with him. She might have been connected to other members as well.

At least nothing the woman had told them would have been eavesdropped on because of a listening device. Grayson had called in a favor and managed to get a CSI over to Hanna's to do a search for a bug that Agent Shaw might have planted. Nothing had turned up.

In the grand scheme of things, that didn't seem like a solid victory, but Hanna had been through enough. Jesse hadn't wanted her to feel even more violated because Shaw or someone else had been listening in on their private conversations.

Evan giggled when Hanna repeated some baby babble back to him, and it yanked Jesse from his worries. He hadn't had many moments like this with Hanna and Evan, and he wanted to hold on to them. Wanted to hold on to Hanna, too. That kiss had been a good start in that happening, but he knew he was a long way from this time together being the norm. First, he had to make things safe for them, and then he could start dealing with the more personal aspects of his life.

Hanna's phone dinged, so Jesse took over feeding the baby while she read the message. "It's from my doctor," she told him. "He set me up for a hypnosis appointment day after tomorrow in San Antonio." She shook her head. "I can't go. Not with things so uncertain here."

Jesse had been about to suggest the same thing, but Hanna had already started to reply to the text. Yes, it was important for her to get her memory back, but they could be attacked en route to and from the appointment.

"Going to my house on the ranch is still an option," Jesse ventured.

He didn't need to spell out why he knew she was hesitant to go there, but she didn't immediately dismiss it as she'd done the other time he'd brought it up. "Maybe in the morning," she agreed, though he could see her trying to steady herself for having to face the security gate where Arnie had taken her at gunpoint.

Jesse was about to try to assure her that it would be okay, but his phone rang. Not Unknown Caller, thank God, because he was too tired to deal with a chat with Bull tonight.

"It's Grayson." Jesse let her know. "Should I put it on speaker?" he added, tipping his head to Evan. Of course, their son wouldn't understand what was being said, but Jesse wanted to make sure Hanna was okay with it.

"Speaker," Hanna verified with a nod.

"Please tell me you have good news," Jesse told Grayson when he answered, adding that Hanna was listening.

"Some. We got IDs on the two attackers. The dead guy is Vince Lutz, and the one we have in custody is Jeremy Cowen. Both have records. Both belong to a militia in Oklahoma. Their group apparently did business with the one here."

That explained why the men hadn't looked familiar to Jesse. "Who hired them?"

"Don't know. Not yet. Cowen says he doesn't know, that he was doing Lutz a favor by going to Hanna's."

Jesse bit on the profanity that came with the jolt of anger. "*A favor?*" he snarled. "One that endangered a baby."

Grayson made a sound to indicate he was in perfect agreement with Jesse's anger. "Cowen claims he had no idea that a baby was in the house, that Lutz told him they were just going there to scare somebody who was ratting out members of the militia. He also said it was Lutz who fired the shots, but we're having both men's guns tested."

That was standard procedure, though Jesse didn't care which of them had pulled the trigger. He wanted Cowen to be charged with attempted murder, child endangerment, trespassing and any other charges Grayson could tack onto those.

"Cowen put a stop to the interview when I pressed

him for details about how Lutz and he had gotten those orders," Grayson explained. "He then asked for a lawyer."

It surprised Jesse that the man hadn't lawyered up right away since he'd been caught at the scene, and he'd been armed. With his record, he had to know he was going to land in jail.

"Theo requested Hanna's phone records," Grayson continued a moment later, "and they arrived about a half hour ago. I've been going through them while I'm waiting for Cowen's lawyer to show. Hanna, do you have any recollection of Agent Shaw calling you the day you were shot?"

Jesse could tell from the way her breath stalled that the answer to that was no. "He didn't mention it either."

"Was it a long call?" Hanna asked.

"Twelve minutes, so long enough. I can contact him and ask what you two talked about," Grayson offered.

"Let me do that after we get Evan down for the night," Jesse said. "That way, Hanna will be able to hear what he has to say. I'll let you know, too."

"Thanks. Oh, and just a heads-up, Dad might be coming over there tonight. Melissa ordered Evan a bunch of books and toys, and he might drop them off. He said if it was late, he'd just leave the stuff on the porch."

Well, it wasn't late, not really, but Boone might go the porch route since he'd know that it was already past Evan's bedtime. Still, the hands would alert Jesse that his father had arrived, so he'd go out and have a quick chat with him to try to assure him that he had things under control.

That might or might not be the truth.

Boone had to be feeling the motherlode of guilt right now because he would be blaming himself for what had happened to Hanna. And for what was still happening to her. It wasn't his fault that Arnie had snapped but, like Jesse, he hadn't been able to stop Hanna from getting hurt. That kind of guilt stayed with you.

As Jesse well knew.

Grayson and he ended the call while Hanna took Evan from the high chair and started the nightly routine of getting the baby ready for bed. First, there was a very messy bath with lots of laughter and splashing, and once he was dry and in his footed PJs, Hanna fed him a bottle while Jesse sat in the kitchen and read through Grayson's initial report on the two gunmen.

Even though the background on both men was thorough, Jesse just couldn't see how they'd crossed paths with any of their suspects. Then again, there probably wouldn't be anything obvious that could give the cops that particular link, but there might be something in the financials to show an unusual transfer of funds. After all, hired guns weren't cheap.

He looked up when Hanna came back in, and Jesse saw that she was still looking exhausted. Still looking amazing, too, as she usually did, but he pushed that aside and held up his phone.

"Are you ready for me to call Agent Shaw, or do you need to try to settle first?" he asked.

"Make the call." On a heavy sigh, she sat next to him at the counter. "The problem is I won't know if he's lying about why he contacted me."

"Maybe not, but just hearing what he has to say might trigger something. The way it did when you were talking to your mother."

In hindsight, he wished he'd held back on that reminder because it seemed to add to her weariness. Still, she motioned for him to make the call, so that's what Jesse did. The agent answered on the first ring.

"The sheriff is stonewalling me about talking to the man he has in custody," Shaw immediately groused.

"That's between the sheriff and you," Jesse responded, and he didn't pause even a heartbeat before he continued. "Why did you call Hanna the day she was shot?"

There was a long pause, followed by some muffled profanity. "Well, it wasn't to tell her that I was dirty or that I had ordered a hit on her. Judging from your tone, though, that's what you think."

"I'm not sure what I think yet," Jesse countered. "I just want to know about that call. And FYI, Hanna has remembered some details about it, so don't bother to lie."

Shaw's next pause was significantly longer and Jesse wished he could see the man's face to try to figure out how he was handling the threat. A bogus threat since Hanna didn't actually have memories of that particular conversation.

"I called Hanna because of her mother's connection to Arnie," Shaw finally said. "I thought maybe Hanna had overheard something I could use to start closing down the militia. Bull had been undercover there too long, and he wasn't reporting as regularly as he should have been. I was worried about him."

"And what did I tell you about Arnie and my mother?" Hanna challenged. Despite the fatigue, she'd managed to add a threatening tone to her voice.

"Nothing. That's the truth," Shaw said when Jesse huffed. "Hanna claimed she didn't know her mother had ever been involved with Arnie."

"But you knew," Jesse said. "How'd you find out?"

"Marlene. She mentioned it in an interview I did with her when I was trying to learn if she was aware of any illegal militia activity in the area."

It seemed an odd thing for Marlene to bring up when talking with a federal agent, but maybe Shaw had said something that'd prompted her to include it.

"Funny that you'd talk to Marlene about that and not the Silver Creek sheriff's office," Jesse pointed out.

This time it was Shaw who huffed. "I've already said I was worried about Bull, and I thought I could subtly question Marlene to find out if she thought there'd been a change in her brother's behavior."

"And?" Jesse pressed when Shaw didn't add anything to that.

"She said she had seen some changes in him and

thought he wasn't paying as much attention to his business as he should. Plus, she didn't like that he was keeping company with Arnie."

Considering Arnie's known drug use, that last part made sense. "Did she have any suspicions that he was a deep cover agent?"

"None," Shaw insisted. Then he paused. "Well, none that she shared with me anyway. Bull kept it secret that he was ATF because he always wanted deep cover. He especially wanted to infiltrate this particular militia and put a stop to it. He didn't think an outsider would be trusted as much as someone like him who was from the area."

Or maybe Bull chose it so he could play both sides. The militia had been around for years, maybe even decades, so it was likely that Bull knew more members than just Arnie. He could fake doing his deep cover assignment while profiting big-time from the sale of guns and such. That way, Bull could also make sure the group wasn't about to be brought down.

"When can I interview the man the sheriff has in custody?" Shaw finally asked.

"Again, that's between the sheriff and you," Jesse clarified.

Shaw grumbled something he didn't catch and ended the call. Probably to contact Grayson.

"If Shaw is the one who sent those gunmen here," Hanna said, "he could want to talk to the surviving one to make sure he doesn't rat him out."

Jesse gave a quick nod because that thought had already occurred to him. Shaw wouldn't even have to threaten the guy. Just by showing up, the gunman would know that Shaw could kill him before he talked to the cops.

Hanna leaned closer to him. "You really believe Marlene didn't know her brother was ATF?"

"Hard to say. I'm not sure how close they were, or still are."

But Jesse doubted Bull had traveled in those same *social circles* that Isabel and Marlene did. Even before Bull left Silver Creek, Jesse had always thought of him as a loner, and that impression of him had remained when Bull moved back three years ago.

Hanna's sigh was loaded with fatigue and frustration, but she must have seen he was feeling the same way because she brushed her hand down his arm. A gesture he'd done earlier to try and soothe *her*.

"I hate what's happening," she said, "but I'm glad you're here. I don't think I could get through this without you."

Oh, man. That gave him a punch of émotion. Not of their usual heat. But of the feelings that he'd failed to protect her six months ago, and he couldn't fail Evan and her again.

He stood, pulling her into his arms and brushing one of those chaste, and hopefully comforting, kisses on the top of her head. She didn't melt against him this time though. She stayed a little stiff when she looked up at him. It seemed to Jesse that she had something to say. What, exactly, he didn't know, but she didn't speak.

She kissed him instead.

Her mouth came to his, not some tentative, testing-the-waters gesture. Hanna kissed him the way she had the night they'd had sex. Holding back nothing. Diving right into the fiery-hot attraction.

It didn't take Jesse long to shift from the "guilt/comfort" mode to this and, despite the bad timing, he welcomed it. He needed this from her. The heat, the need. Because it felt like forgiveness, too. As if Hanna might be able to get past what had happened to her. Of course, that could be all wishful thinking on his part.

Soon, he wasn't able to think at all because she deepened the kiss and dragged him closer, tightening her grip around him. Jesse took things from there. He did some dragging of his own so he could feel her body against his. So he could take in her scent. Her taste. So he could deepen the kiss and cause the heat to skyrocket.

Even though Hanna likely couldn't remember this, Jesse experienced some déjà vu. The instant, soaring need. This fire that blazed between them. Suddenly, they couldn't get close enough to each other, and the deep kisses were fueling the flames higher and higher until he had to have more than just her mouth. Jesse slid his hand between them, cupped her breast and swiped his thumb over her nipple.

Hanna made a familiar sound. A low, throaty moan that revved up his body even more. Of course, he hadn't needed that, not with this primal ache spreading through him. An ache demanding that he take her now, now, now. But thankfully he managed to hold on to a shred of common sense.

And that's why he broke the kiss, why he quit touching her, and he pulled back.

"I can take you to bed," he said, looking her straight in the eyes, "but I have to make sure it's what you want. Not what your body wants," he amended when she gave a dry laugh. "I just don't want you to have any regrets."

Oh, it'd cost him to say all of that, and a certain part of his body thought he was pretty damn stupid to even bring it up. But this was Hanna, the mother of his son. The woman he was certain he loved. A round of sex would no doubt be amazing and burn off some of this fatigue, but he couldn't have it putting up more barriers between them if Hanna regretted it. There'd been enough barriers, and this dangerous situation had helped lower them. Jesse wanted to keep them down, and maybe, just maybe, they could have a future together.

He could see the debate she was having with her own body, but she didn't get a chance to voice her decision because his phone rang. The sound was a jolt that broke the tension, and the moment was lost. Since it could be Grayson with an update, or one of the hands reporting a problem, Jesse had no choice but to drag his phone from his pocket. But it wasn't them. Unknown Caller was on the screen.

"Bull," he grumbled. Jesse so wasn't in the mood to deal with him tonight, but he set up the record function and answered the call.

"I had no part in this," Bull immediately said. "I want you to know that."

"No part in what?" Jesse demanded.

"Your father. Boone," Bull blurted. "He's on his way to Hanna's place, and somebody's going to try to kidnap him."

Jesse threw off the slam of worry and anger. "Who's going to try to do that?" he roared.

"Not sure, but you need to get him some help fast." That was it; the only info Bull gave him before he ended the call.

Jesse quickly pressed his father's number, and his stomach muscles hardened when Boone didn't answer. "Call Grayson and let him know what Bull just said," he instructed Hanna, and he kept listening to the rings, kept praying, until Boone finally answered.

The relief came.

But it was short-lived when Jesse heard Boone's voice.

"I was driving to Hanna's when somebody plowed into the side of my truck," Boone said, his words rushing together. "It was one of those big SUVs, and it flew out from one of the ranch trails. He tried to run me off the road."

Hell. It was true. Someone was after his father. "Are you all right? Were you hurt?"

"I'm okay. I didn't stop or end up in the ditch, but neither did the SUV. It's following me, and I don't want to take this to Hanna's doorstep."

Jesse didn't especially want that either, but it was their best option. "There's a deputy and ranch hands here. I'll alert them that you'll be driving in. I don't think the SUV will come onto the grounds once they see the armed men."

At least, he hoped they wouldn't, and he put his father on hold while he texted Miguel Navarro to let him know that trouble might be arriving soon.

"Grayson's on the way," Hanna relayed once Jesse was back on the line with his father.

Good, because that meant they could maybe sandwich in the SUV and find out who the hell was behind this. But just in case the person or persons behind the kidnapping scheme started shooting, Jesse had to tell Hanna something that was going to put the fear right back in her eyes.

"You'll need to take Evan into the bathroom again," he said.

She nodded, sucked in a hard breath and hurried in that direction. Since she knew the drill, she'd secure and stay down, but Jesse hated to have to put Hanna and the baby through this again.

Jesse whipped his attention back to the phone when he heard the loud crash. "The SUV rammed into my truck again," Boone reported.

That tightened every muscle in Jesse's body, and he had a too vivid image of his father fighting the steering wheel just to stay on the road. It twisted away at Jesse that he couldn't storm out to help him, but that could be a fatal mistake for Hanna and Evan. Because whoever was doing this could want to use this to get to them.

"How far out are you?" Jesse asked, trying to keep

his voice level. He hurried to the window to keep watch.

"A half mile," Boone answered just as Jesse heard another loud bang. The sound of metal crunching into metal. The SUV had plowed into him again.

Boone was no doubt going as fast as he could on the rural road, and that meant he would be here in only a couple of minutes. Minutes that would no doubt feel like an eternity.

"Can you describe the SUV?" Jesse asked. It was info he needed, but he also wanted to hear his father's voice, to make sure he wasn't hurt and was still capable of talking.

"A black Chevy Suburban, late model, with a reinforced bumper. I tried to get a look at the license plate, but it's been smeared with mud or something."

It didn't surprise him that his father had noticed all of that—even while he was under attack. Boone was in a family of lawmen, and he wasn't the sort to panic. Good thing, because it was obvious he was in grave danger.

"I'm guessing they obscured the license plate since it can be traced back to somebody who doesn't want to be traced. Or else it's stolen, and they don't want the cops seeing it and trying to pull them over," Boone added, and he was spot-on with that theory.

There was another loud crash, and Jesse heard his father ground out some profanity. He also heard the squeal of tires. He couldn't see the end of Hanna's driveway because of the trees, but this had to be his father. Well, unless the would-be kidnappers had sent another team to try to get to Hanna and him. Either way, Jesse drew his gun and went to the door. He disarmed the security system so he could open it and take aim.

That's when Jesse heard something else he darn sure didn't want to hear.

Gunfire.

Two shots had come from the vicinity of the end of the driveway, and he prayed the bullets hadn't hit his father. Seconds later, Boone's familiar red truck came into sight. He didn't stop in front of the house though. His father continued past to the far side of the property, to a cluster of trees. A position he'd no doubt chosen because it would keep the gunfire away from the house.

And on him.

Boone could be gunned down.

Jesse stepped out from cover, his gaze firing toward the other end of the driveway where the SUV could be approaching. But it wasn't. Just the opposite. There was a slash of headlights cutting through the darkness, and that's when he knew the vehicle was turning around. Trying to escape.

Again, Jesse had to fight the overwhelming urge to go after them and make them pay for what they'd just tried to do. But he couldn't take that risk. Besides, these could be more henchmen, like the one Grayson already had in custody, and there was too much at stake with Hanna and Evan for him to go after a long shot.

"I'm okay," his father assured him when he got out

of his truck. Boone had a gun, and he was already taking aim down the driveway. So were two of the ranch hands and the reserve deputy. "They're running away like the cowards they are," Boone grumbled.

Cowards who didn't mind killing or endangering the life of a baby.

Yeah, they were going to pay. Jesse wasn't sure how to make that happen, not yet, but he'd figure out a way.

"I'm real sorry about this," Boone said, limping his way toward Jesse.

The apology riled Jesse because it wasn't necessary. This wasn't his father's fault. He'd simply gotten caught up in the crosshairs of this mess. But the limp cooled Jesse's anger.

"You said you weren't hurt," Jesse pointed out.

"I'm not. I just banged my knee when the cowards rammed into me. Are Hanna and Evan all right?"

Jesse nodded. Well, they were as all right as they could be. Hanna was probably terrified and huddled in the bathtub with Evan.

"Let Grayson know what happened once he gets here," Jesse shouted out to the deputy and the hands. Grayson would likely want to go in pursuit of the SUV or at least make some calls for a BOLO on the vehicle. He rattled off the specs Boone had given him so Grayson would know what he was looking for.

"And tell Grayson I'm not hurt," Boone added so that his son wouldn't worry. But Jesse intended to verify that Boone was indeed unharmed.

Jesse got Boone inside the house as fast as he could and shut the door so he could reset the security system. He didn't want a hired thug trying to sneak through one of the windows while the alarm was off.

"So, what the heck just happened?" Boone immediately asked. "Who tried to run me off the road?"

"I don't know, but it's possible we can get something from the man Grayson has in custody. I'm pretty sure somebody in the militia is behind this."

Boone shook his head in disgust, but he obviously wasn't surprised. Everything that had gone on seemed to lead right back to the militia and their illegal activities.

"Let me tell Hanna what's going on," Jesse said, but he'd barely made it a step when he glanced out the window and saw the bobbing of headlights coming up the driveway.

Jesse drew the gun he'd just holstered. Beside him, Boone did the same.

"It's probably just Grayson," Boone muttered.

But one look at the vehicle and Jesse knew that it wasn't. This was an old blue truck, and when it came to a stop, the hands and the deputy all took aim.

"It's me," someone shouted. "Don't shoot."

Jesse watched as Bull stepped out. He put his hands on his head and stayed in place.

"Don't shoot," Bull called out again. "I'm here to surrender."

Chapter Twelve

Hanna eased Evan back into his crib and stood there to make sure he was truly asleep. He was. In fact, he'd hardly stirred when she'd made the mad rush earlier to get him into the bathroom when Boone was being attacked. Evan had stayed asleep through the entire ordeal and maybe that would continue while they got through the next couple of hours.

When Jesse had come into the bathroom to tell her it was safe to leave and that his father was okay, he'd given her the shocking news that Bull had come to her house to surrender. Hanna had no idea if that was true or if this was some kind of ploy on his part. If it was a ruse, though, she figured that Jesse would keep things under control.

She could hear the murmur of voices at the front of the house. Jesse's, Boone's. And Bull's. Yes, he was actually in her house. The man who'd been part of her nearly being killed was here.

Just yards away.

Jesse had explained that was necessary since he didn't want to be standing out in the open with Bull while waiting for Grayson and backup to arrive, and that none of the vehicles on scene were bullet resistant since the reserve deputy had come in his own truck. Hanna hadn't wanted Jesse or Boone at risk like that, either, but she was certain she had surprised Jesse when she'd told him she had wanted to speak to Bull. This wasn't just about confronting her fears or facing her nightmares. She wanted some answers, and she hoped that Bull would give them to her.

Hanna started out of the nursery, but her phone vibrated with an incoming call. She glanced at the screen, saw that it was her mother and considered letting it go to voice mail. But then she sighed and answered it because it was possible Isabel had heard about the attempted kidnapping and wanted to make sure Evan and she hadn't been hurt.

"We're okay," Hanna said the moment she answered.

"Why wouldn't you be?" Isabel asked just as quickly. "Did something else happen?"

Hanna groaned and mentally kicked herself. She decided not to hold back the truth since Isabel would hear about it anyway. Or maybe she already knew and this call was about playing the "I'm innocent" routine.

"Someone tried to kidnap Boone," Hanna explained. "He got away."

She didn't add the rest about Bull showing up and surrendering to Jesse. Best to keep that under wraps until Bull was actually away from the house and behind bars. Hanna didn't want to give hired guns, or anyone else, a reason to come here looking for the man.

"See, the Rylands are magnets for trouble," Isabel grumbled. "I know things aren't good between us right now, but I wish you'd bring Evan here where you'll both be safe."

Hanna so didn't have time for this. And she wasn't putting on the kid gloves to give Isabel a kind response. "You're right. Things aren't good between us right now, and it's because you didn't tell me the truth."

"I didn't tell you because I thought it would upset you," Isabel argued. "And it did. Listen, if you want me to feel bad because I was involved with Arnie, then know that I feel bad. I'm sorry I ever met the man, sorry that I talked to him, and I'm especially sorry that he almost killed you."

Hanna wanted to say "Good" and end the call, but she reminded herself that her mother might not be a devious criminal. She might only be guilty of bad judgment with a bad man. So that's why she eased back on her tone.

"I have to go," Hanna said. "We'll talk soon."

Isabel didn't try to change her mind or stay on the line. She simply muttered a goodbye and ended the call.

Hanna tucked the baby monitor in her pocket and, after a few deep breaths, made her way from the nursery to the living room. She immediately spotted Bull. He was kneeling on the floor with his hands tucked behind his head while Jesse and Boone kept guns trained on him.

Jesse looked over at her when he heard her footsteps, and she saw the instant disapproval on his face. He hadn't wanted her to go through this. Hadn't thought it was necessary. And he might be right. This could all be for nothing.

Bull's gaze met hers, too, and he didn't sneer or snarl, as she'd expected. In fact, there was nothing defiant about his expression or body language.

"I'm sorry," Bull immediately said.

She didn't ask if he was apologizing for the shooting or because of all the other havoc. Instead, she looked at Jesse. "How did Bull know someone would try to kidnap Boone?" she asked.

"He claims he got the info through a militia member he's still in contact with. A guy named Hector Ames."

"It's true," Bull insisted, but neither Boone nor Jesse spared him a glance. "Hector's not happy with some of the things the militia has done, so I've stayed in touch with him."

"Grayson will be pulling Hector in for a chat about that very soon," Jesse added.

"Where's Grayson?" Hanna wanted to know.

"He went in pursuit of the SUV, and he followed it out to the interstate where he lost it. He's making his way back here so he can transport Bull to jail."

"The Silver Creek jail," Bull insisted. "You can't turn me over to federal custody because I'm not sure who I can trust."

"Welcome to the club," Hanna mumbled, but that wasn't exactly true. She knew she could trust Jesse,

Boone and the other Rylands. She just wasn't so sure about everyone else.

Especially Bull.

Leveling her breathing as much as she could, Hanna walked closer to stand shoulder to shoulder with Jesse so she could stare down at Bull. Facing her own personal bogeyman.

"Tell me what happened the night I was shot," she said, and it wasn't a request. It was a demand.

Bull ground out a single word of raw profanity. "I was hoping you could tell me. I was hoping you'd gotten your memory back."

"I regained some of it," she told him and went with the threat she'd already used. "Enough of it that I'll know if you're lying."

Bull groaned. "You need to remember all of it. Because I'm damn sure you saw or heard something I didn't."

Maybe she had. That's what her gut was telling her anyway. But nothing she'd done so far had caused those particular memories to return. Perhaps talking with Bull would help with that.

"Go over everything that happened," Hanna insisted.

"I didn't lie when I was taken into custody," Bull argued. "I just didn't include certain things. Like the fact that I was ATF, because someone would have killed me right off. Somebody in the militia would have gotten to me, and since I didn't know who was pulling the strings there, I wouldn't have been able to watch my back."

"Everything that happened that night," she repeated. "I want to hear it."

Obviously, Bull had wanted her to be the one to provide the answers. Exactly what answers, she didn't know, but he was going to have to wait on that. Maybe forever if her memory never fully returned.

"Like I told Jesse, the sheriff, and every ATF agent and deputy who asked me after I was arrested, Arnie called me that night to say he was going to the ranch to have it out with Boone and Jesse. He was certain he was about to be arrested."

"He was," Jesse verified. "So were you and any other militia members we could round up."

"Yeah, well, Arnie had gotten wind of that, and he was spitting mad. And high. Not a good combination, so I told him to pick me up and we'd go together. I thought I could talk him out of doing something stupid." Bull paused, cursed again. "Needless to say, I failed."

"Yes, you did," Hanna agreed. "Keep going."

Bull didn't dodge her gaze, but his jaw muscles were tight and flexing. "I tried to calm Arnie down by saying we should go get a beer or something and work out a plan. That if we just showed up at the security gate, the hands probably wouldn't let us onto the ranch. But Arnie said we'd just break down the gate or go over the fence. He was determined to get to Boone and you."

Jesse huffed. "And at this point you didn't think to call me? Or Grayson? Or your handler in the ATF to warn us of Arnie's intentions?"

"I didn't know if I could trust you to keep it quiet that I was deep cover."

"You could have," Jesse assured him. "We aren't dirty cops."

"No, but I didn't know that, did I? And, as for my handler…well, that was Shaw." Bull snarled. "No way was I going to trust him."

"Why not?" Jesse pressed, but he held up his hand to put the pause on Bull's answer when they all heard a vehicle stop in front of the house. "Grayson's here."

Boone kept his gun trained on Bull while Jesse went to the door to let in the sheriff. Grayson stepped in, and he made a sweeping glance around the room.

"Are Evan and you all right?" Grayson asked her.

Hanna nodded, and Grayson did a repeat of the question to his dad. Boone nodded, too, but when Grayson glanced down at Boone's leg, Hanna knew that someone, probably Jesse, had told him of their father's possible injury. She was betting Boone would soon be making a trip to the ER to be examined.

"Bull here was just telling us how he already knew he couldn't trust Shaw the night Hanna was shot. Oh, and FYI, I read him the Miranda again in case he forgot his rights."

That earned Jesse a brief scowl from Bull, but obviously the man wanted to get on with his account. "I couldn't confide in Shaw because I thought maybe he'd made some side deals with the militia. There was talk that an insider was looking out for them. Things like making sure they were warned of a raid before it happened. That sort of warning could have come from someone in the ATF."

"It could have come from other people, too," Jesse pointed out. "But you zoomed in on Shaw. Any proof of one of those side deals?"

"None. I was trying to get the truth when Arnie went off the deep end and stormed out to your family's ranch."

"A ranch where I just happened to be," Hanna remarked. "What made Arnie go after me and pull me out of my car?"

Bull hesitated again, but he didn't seem to be trying to come up with a story she'd buy. Then again, he was a trained federal agent, a deep cover one, so he had been trained to lie.

"Did it have anything to do with my mother?" she straightforwardly asked.

She carefully watched Bull for his reaction, and what she didn't see was surprise. "Arnie mentioned that he'd talked to your mother," Bull finally said. "He didn't say about what." He stopped again, stared at her. "You think your mother had something to do with Arnie shooting you?"

"Do you?" she countered just as fast.

"No." But there was doubt in his voice. "Did Isabel have anything to do with what happened?"

"I'm not sure," she admitted. "What did Arnie say about the talk he'd had with her?"

Bull shook his head in a gesture to indicate he was thinking about that. "Nothing specific. He said something about Isabel having called him and he went over to see her. They had drinks. Gin and tonics," he added. "He said they were strong, and he was woozy when he left."

Hanna glanced at Jesse and saw that he had the same question she did. Had Isabel drugged Arnie? Of course, she wouldn't have actually had to hide the drugs since Arnie was a user, but maybe Isabel had given him enough booze, drugs, or a combination of them, in the hope that he'd go after Jesse.

And that was what he did.

The theory fit. Well, it did if she could actually wrap her mind around the image of the prim and snobby Isabel setting up something so sinister. Hanna wasn't quite able to do that, but it didn't mean she believed Isabel was innocent. At a minimum, she'd provoked Arnie. It was possible she'd incited him so that he'd no longer known what he was doing.

"Other than Arnie, I never heard any of the other militia members talk about Isabel," Bull volunteered. He was still staring at her. "But if you think she was connected, then I need to know."

"Who did the militia members talk about?" Jesse asked Bull before Hanna had to answer. Good thing, too, since she hadn't been sure what to say.

Bull huffed and adjusted his position on the floor. He continued to keep his hands tucked behind his head. "You've arrested the big guns of the operation, and I've already given you Hector's name."

"But you haven't given us the biggest name," Grayson interjected. "You haven't told us who's actually running it."

"Because I don't know," Bull snapped. He repeated it, but this time there wasn't anger in his voice but rather frustration.

Hanna didn't want to empathize with the man she'd feared and hated all these months, but she did on that one point. Until they knew the identity of the person running this deadly show, none of them would be safe. Bull included. Because she believed him when he'd said that someone would try to kill him. The head of the militia would want him dead for sure. Maybe a dirty agent like Shaw would as well.

"Go over the rest of what happened that night," Jesse prompted when the room fell silent. "You and Arnie arrived at the gate to the ranch, and you saw Hanna. Why'd Arnie take her from her car?"

"Did I say something to provoke him?" Hanna added, and that caused Jesse to look at her. He was silently assuring her that she hadn't been responsible in any way, but Bull's expression said differently.

"I don't know for sure," Bull admitted. "You said something to him when he threw open the passenger's-side door, but I suspect you just asked him what the heck he was doing. Or something along those lines. Before that, he was ranting and carrying on, and then the next thing I knew, he bolted out of his truck and ran to your car. He pulled the gun and had you in a chokehold before I could stop him."

Since those were the images on the security camera, Hanna had no problem reliving those moments, and even though her mind had blocked out the actual memories, she could sense down to the bone the fear she'd felt. She had been terrified for her baby.

"Then what?" Jesse insisted. There was fresh anger in his voice now, no doubt because he was reliving all of this right along with her. He'd been terrified for Evan, too. And her. She didn't need memories to know that.

Bull took a long breath before he answered. "Arnie tried to take Hanna back to his truck, but he dropped his keys. He was mumbling and cursing, and when we heard someone from the ranch coming to the gate, he said we had to get the hell out of there. I didn't think he meant to drag Hanna along. I figured he'd just start running for the woods, but he took her."

"And you didn't stop him," Jesse snapped.

"It happened fast, and I didn't want to get into a struggle with him because I was afraid the gun would go off. Hell, by then Arnie had it aimed at her head."

"The gun did go off," Hanna noted pointedly.

Bull nodded, sighed. "Within seconds after we got into that thick cluster of trees. It was dark, so I don't know if the shooting was an accident. I think it was," he added, not sounding convinced of that either. "You fell, and Arnie went into a full panic. He was going to pull the trigger again, he said so you wouldn't be able to tell anyone he'd been the one to shoot you. That's when I shot and killed him."

Hanna studied his face and went through all of that word by word. She so wished she had a lie detector to know if Bull was telling the truth or if something else had gone on. She knew from reading the reports that the lab had matched the bullets. The one in her head to Arnie's weapon. The one in Arnie to Bull's gun. So that meshed with the story Bull had told, but again her gut said Bull was leaving something out.

"I know something else happened," Hanna insisted, and it wasn't a bluff this time. "Tell me."

Bull certainly didn't jump to deny that. "I'm pretty sure somebody else was there in those trees. Somebody other than you, me and Arnie."

Both Grayson and Boone muttered some profanity. They were obviously angry and disgusted that Bull hadn't told them this earlier.

"Who?" Jesse challenged.

"I didn't see the person," Bull insisted, "but I got a glimpse of a gun. Aimed at me. I dropped to the ground, trying to get into a position to defend myself, when you and your cousin arrived on scene. The person must have run off."

"And what reason do you have for not telling us this before now?" Jesse asked, his question filled with sarcasm and anger.

"Because I thought it was Shaw," Bull admitted. "Because if I'd told you I believed it was him, then I'd have to explain how I knew an ATF agent. I didn't want my cover blown. I figured it was best if I kept on letting everyone believe I was in the militia so I could keep gathering info about the leader."

"You thought it was Shaw," Jesse muttered. "Was it him?"

"I had my lawyer ask him. I couldn't talk to Shaw myself because I didn't want anyone making the connection between him and me. Anyway, Shaw said no, that he wasn't there that night."

"You believe him?" Hanna asked.

Bull stayed quiet a long time. "Yeah. About that anyway. I still think he could be dirty and playing both sides of this, but to the best of my knowledge, Shaw didn't know that Arnie would be going to the Silver Creek Ranch. There's only one person who for sure knew that Arnie would be going to the ranch to confront Boone and Jesse."

Everything inside Hanna tightened. "My mother?"

Bull shook his head. "I don't think she knew the timing of when Arnie would be there. Could be wrong and Arnie might have told her he was heading straight for the ranch when they were drinking. But someone else knew." He paused again. "My sister, Marlene."

Chapter Thirteen

Marlene.

Jesse didn't like that the woman's name kept coming up in connection with the shooting and the militia. But Bull obviously thought the connection was there.

"How would Marlene have known that you and Arnie would be at the ranch at that specific time?" Jesse demanded.

"Because I told her," Bull admitted. "She was at my place when Arnie called, and she would have heard me trying to calm him down. I specifically told him not to go to the ranch, and we argued about it. It wouldn't have taken much for her to piece together where we were going when Arnie got to my house."

No, it wouldn't have taken much, but Jesse still wasn't convinced. "If you're saying your sister followed Arnie and you, and that she aimed a gun at you, then you must believe she's part of the militia."

Bull's jaw went to iron. "She very well could be. I just don't know." He groaned, cursed. "I don't want to believe she'd kill me, or anyone for that matter, but she might have considered it if she found out I was an agent. Or if she thought I was going to rat out the militia."

Again, Jesse wasn't convinced, but he had no intention of dismissing Bull's theory. If Marlene was involved in the militia, she might indeed have wanted to silence anyone who could have spilled secrets about the illegal operations in the group. In her mind, both Bull and Arnie could have done just that if they'd been arrested and interrogated.

"Anything else you want to ask him?" Grayson offered, glancing first at Hanna, then at Jesse and finally at Boone. When the three of them shook their heads, Grayson took out his handcuffs. "All right, then I'll go ahead and get Bull to jail." He put the cuffs on Bull's wrists.

"You won't be doing that alone," Jesse insisted.

Grayson tipped his head to the driveway. "Ava and Theo are already waiting out there, and they'll be my backup. I'm leaving the ranch hands and a reserve deputy here in case there's another round of trouble. If you need more ranch hands, just let me know," he added to Jesse.

"Wait," Bull said when Grayson hauled him to his feet. "I've got a plan. It's risky, but hell, just about everything we do at this point will be."

"What plan?" Again, Jesse didn't bother to tone down the skepticism.

Bull glanced at Grayson. "Are you sure you can stop someone from trying to kill me when I'm behind bars?"

Grayson gave him a flat look. "You'll be protected.

Neither I nor any of my deputies has ties to the militia."

He said that with complete confidence because Jesse knew it was true. Like Grayson, he trusted every one of his fellow lawmen with his life. They'd die if it came to protecting a prisoner. Even someone like Bull.

"Then, let's go with that," Bull continued. "You'll guarantee protection, and I'll lay the groundwork to draw this snake out. Even if that snake happens to be my sister." He tacked that last bit on in a mumble. His gaze connected with Grayson's again. "You'll get the word out that I'm in custody and am cooperating. *Fully cooperating*," Bull emphasized. "And that I intend to spill previously undisclosed info about the militia."

Grayson stood there, obviously considering that from all angles. Jesse did the same, and he could see a huge potential problem. If someone sent an army of thugs to the sheriff's office, there could be a gunfight. And a bloodbath. Obviously though, that was something Grayson would consider.

"Can you lock down the entire building where you'll have me jailed?" Bull wanted to know.

"I can," Grayson confirmed. "The windows are all bulletproof, and the doors are metal and can be fully secured. Along with the cops inside, my stepbrother and cousin are Texas Rangers. I could have them positioned on top of the nearby buildings. They could spot anyone approaching."

"Good. Do that," Bull insisted. "Get everything in

place and then let it leak that I'm ready to give you everything, including names, and that I'll do that as soon as my lawyer shows up."

In theory, that would give the militia leader time to launch an attack to silence Bull before he could rat them out, but Jesse saw another flaw in the plan. "The leader might not show. Not if he or she has henchmen to send."

Bull nodded. "Yeah, but then the sheriff here will have at least some of those henchmen in custody, and he could pressure one of them to cough up the name of their boss."

Grayson looked at Jesse, no doubt to get his take on whether or not doing this was worth the risk. It was. Because if it worked, Hanna and Evan might finally be safe. As long as the leader was out there pulling the strings, then none of them could ever get on with their lives.

"It's a solid plan," Bull argued. "And if I'm going to put my life at risk, I'd rather do it while I'm in the custody of someone I can trust."

"How do you know you can trust us?" Jesse quickly countered.

Bull looked him straight in the eyes. "Because if you'd wanted me dead, I already would be."

That brought on a fresh round of anger for Jesse. "Oh, I still want you dead for the part you played in Hanna and my son nearly being killed, but I'm not a killer. Besides, I think you're right about using a fake confession to draw out the ring leader in all of this."

Jesse gave Grayson a confirming nod, and that

was all it took to get him moving Bull toward the door. "I'll text you when I have everything in place and we're ready to do this leak. It'll probably be at least a couple of hours. I don't think this will cause any henchmen to come here for Hanna and you, but better safe than sorry. Be on the lookout for any and everything once I put it out there that Bull is selling out the group."

"I will. Good luck," Jesse added under his breath.

He hated that Hanna's and Evan's safety came down to such a thing like luck, but it was definitely going to play into this. Of course, there were no guarantees that the militia leader would take the bait. He or she might see this for what it was.

A ploy.

But so far, the leader had made some reckless moves by sending thugs to Hanna's and by trying to kidnap Boone. Maybe the recklessness would continue and by morning, Grayson would have enough people in custody that they could finally get to the truth.

"You're riding with Ava and Theo," Grayson told Boone. "And you'll be taking a trip to the ER to have that leg checked out. Please," he added, no doubt when he saw an argument about that spark in Boone's eyes.

Boone finally nodded, and he turned his attention to Jesse. "If you need anything, just let me know." He extended that offer to Hanna by glancing at her as well. "FYI, I got the books and toys for Evan in my truck. I didn't forget, but since it's not a good idea to get them out, they'll have to wait. Stay safe," he added to both of them.

"We will," Jesse assured him, and he went with Grayson, Bull and Boone to the door.

Jesse didn't close it right away. He stood by, keeping watch with his hand over his gun in case goons were out there waiting for Bull to make an appearance. But all was quiet as Grayson secured Bull in the cruiser and Boone got in with Ava and Theo. As soon as they'd driven away, Jesse did the lockup and armed the security system.

Since he'd already checked, he knew there was an armed ranch hand on every side of the house. The reserve deputy was keeping watch in the driveway. Added to that, they could have extra men out here in less than ten minutes. So, all the bases were covered.

And that left Hanna.

One look at her and he could tell that she was beyond exhausted. So was he, and since Grayson had said it would be a couple of hours before he'd be ready to leak Bull's fake confession, then it was Hanna's best shot at getting in a nap. Especially since Evan was already asleep. Jesse confirmed that by glancing at the monitor she still had clasped in her hand.

He put his palm on the small of her back to lead her to the nursery, he knew there was no way she'd be using her own bedroom. "I promise I'll wake you when I get word from Grayson."

Then, as a precaution, he might go ahead and have her move back into the bathroom with Evan. Jesse didn't want to tell her that now, though, since he doubted she'd be able to sleep with that weighing on her. Of course, sleep might not happen anyway, but he wanted her to give it a try.

She stopped in the doorway of the nursery, gave Evan a glance no doubt to assure herself that he was still okay. He was. And then she turned back to Jesse. "You'll get some rest, too?"

"Absolutely," he lied.

Clearly, he didn't convince her that was anywhere near the truth because the corner of her mouth lifted in a dry smile. "Then, since we'll both likely be awake, why don't you stay in the nursery with Evan and me? The lounge chair in there pulls out into a twin bed. Please," she added in a pleading tone that was similar to the one Grayson had used on Boone.

Jesse didn't hesitate with his nod. No way would he turn her down, not when his being there might give her even a shred of comfort. Still, this was Hanna, and the idea of sleeping next to her, in a small bed, no less, had his exhausted body coming up with a whole different idea to help them relax.

A really bad idea.

Of course, bad ideas just always seemed to come to mind whenever he was this close to Hanna, and it didn't help that he hadn't fully cooled down from their earlier kissing session. Being next to her would be torture. The good, cheap thrills kind, but he'd just have to keep himself in check.

Or not.

Jesse immediately rethought that notion the moment they stepped inside the nursery. When Hanna slipped her hand around the back of his neck, pulled him down to her.

And kissed him.

HANNA HAD DECIDED on the kiss the moment Jesse had given her the nod about staying in the nursery with her. Of course, it hadn't been a nod of approval for them to launch into another make-out session, but she knew he'd be willing. Willing to give her a lot more than just kisses and comforting hugs.

Jesse wanted her.

She could see that want, that heat, in his eyes every time he looked at her, and each time it was somewhat of a surprise. After she'd basically rejected him and had likely crushed his heart, he still hadn't given up on her. She didn't deserve that kind of blind loyalty, but that didn't stop her from accepting it.

Because she wanted Jesse, too.

For months, she had tried to deny this fire between them. In part because of her mother's harping and also because she hadn't remembered exactly how it'd been between them. But now it no longer mattered if she recalled the memories that she'd made with Jesse when they'd had sex. What mattered were the memories they made right now.

Of course, this could turn out to be a huge mistake. One they'd both end up regretting. It would certainly complicate a situation that was always riddled with complications, but she was past the point of no return. Past the point of worrying about the consequences. She needed Jesse. He needed her. And she was going to take everything from him that he was willing to give her.

The heat from the kiss helped her confirm she was making the right decision to be with him. Even if it was just for this night. This moment. Even if it became their second "one and only."

Jesse didn't seem to question her decision. Maybe because the scalding attraction and need didn't give him a choice about that either. He just sank into the kiss, deepening it while he pulled her closer to him.

She felt the hard muscles of his chest against her breasts and her nipples tightened in response to the contact. Jesse upped that contact to the next level. Without breaking the kiss, he slid his hand under her shirt, pushed down the cups of her bra and touched her.

Hanna tried and failed to silence the moan that came from deep within her throat. The moan that no doubt told Jesse just how much that fueled the heat. He seemed to know her body and he definitely knew how to use his fingers to draw out every ounce of pleasure.

Then he drew out even more.

He lowered his head, took one of her nipples into his mouth. This time she didn't moan. She gasped, and Hanna took hold of his hair to anchor him in place. Not that he seemed to have intentions of going anywhere, but she didn't want to lose these wild sensations that were firing through every inch of her body.

Jesse kept up the kissing while he backed her toward the chair. He broke the contact only long enough to pull her shirt over her head. Her bra went, too, and this time when he returned to her nipple, he used his tongue.

The pleasure just kept flooding her. Until a thought flashed into her head, that is.

"Do you have a condom?" she asked, remembering full well that it hadn't stopped her from getting pregnant with Evan. "Please tell me you have one."

"I do, in my wallet." Jesse stopped, though, and met her gaze and waited. No doubt to make sure that a condom was enough for her to go through with what was about to happen.

It was.

And she didn't think that decision was because her body was on fire. All right, that played into it, but she reasoned that the odds were in their favor. Since they'd had one failed condom before meant they likely weren't going to have another. She could hope so anyway.

Hanna set the baby monitor on the table next to them, pulled Jesse back to her, and this time she was the one who went deep with the kiss.

He responded, all right.

It was as if a leash on his willpower loosened inside him and he eased her back in the lounger while he lowered the kisses to her stomach. Again, he hit all the right spots, and his breath was now so close to the front of her jeans that she felt herself soften. Her body, preparing for what it was insisting Jesse give her.

Jesse's body was all-in on this, too, and she had no

trouble feeling his erection pressing behind the zipper of his jeans when he made his way back up her body to reclaim her mouth. She welcomed the kiss, the heat, but it revved up the need, and she knew she wanted more.

She started with his shirt.

Fumbling, she somehow managed to get it unbuttoned, and she shoved it off him. She immediately pulled him to her so she could feel his warm bare skin against hers. Yes, this was what she wanted, but like the kisses, it only upped the urgency.

Jesse must have felt that urgency because he went after her jeans. Obviously, his hands were steadier than hers because he got her unsnapped and unzipped, and he shimmied off her shoes and the jeans. Her panties went next.

And Jesse started a different round of kisses.

Right in the center of her body.

Hanna nearly climaxed then and there at the touch of his mouth on such a sensitive spot. She couldn't remember ever having sensations this intense. And maybe she never had. But she suspected it'd happened with Jesse a year and a half ago when they'd landed in bed.

"More," she heard herself murmur. "I want you naked now."

Jesse obliged her. Well, he did after giving her a few more of those well-placed, mind-blowing kisses. He stood and retrieved the condom from his wallet before he shoved his jeans and boxers down over his hips.

Hanna silently cursed the nearly dark room, and

she wished she had more than the night-light so she could take a better look at him. But what she could see confirmed that Jesse was indeed a hot cowboy, both clothed and naked.

He settled back on the lounger and robbed Hanna of her breath while he got the condom on. The lounger wasn't wide or especially suited for having sex, but they were past the point of needing comfort. They only needed each other.

And Jesse gave her exactly that.

He was gentle when he pushed inside her. Obviously holding back so he didn't hurt her. But Hanna tried to rid him of any doubts about that when she hooked her legs around his back and lifted her hips. The leash inside snapped again and he started the hard thrusts that would eventually give her the pleasure and relief from the pressure-cooker heat building inside her.

She heard him whisper her name, felt his warm breath on her neck when he repeated it. And that was the final piece she needed to feel herself go over the edge. She buried her face against him and let go.

Moments later, Jesse followed her.

Chapter Fourteen

Jesse held Hanna while she thankfully got some sleep. Apparently, good sex was a cure for frayed nerves. A temporary cure anyway. The calm certainly wouldn't last, but he'd hang on to it as long as he could. Every peaceful moment he could give her was a gift. Unfortunately, it was probably also the calm before the storm.

Once Grayson had the plan set in motion, there was no telling what would happen, and it might be a long time before they had any kind of peace and quiet again. A long time, too, before he could be sure that Hanna and Evan were safe.

Across the room, he could hear the soft sounds of Evan's breathing, and it occurred to him that many parents probably had this. Great sex and the comfort of being with their child. Of course, most probably didn't go for that great sex in the nursery, but his son was none the wiser, and it almost certainly lessened the tension for them to be so close to him.

Hanna would no doubt have second thoughts about what they'd just done. Might even worry about another unplanned pregnancy. But for now she would have these moments, and it appeared she had fallen into a deep, restful sleep. She wasn't shifting or muttering from nightmares despite the cramped space on the lounger, so Jesse stayed still, too, despite the urgency building inside him to keep digging into the investigation. He could be only one piece of evidence away from finding out who'd been responsible for all this misery and havoc.

His phone dinged with a text, and even though it was a soft sound, it blared out like a security alarm in the otherwise quiet room. Hanna woke with a jolt, jackknifing in the lounger, and she seemed ready to jump into the middle of a fierce battle. She settled down, though, when her eyes met his and leveled out even more when she glanced at Evan and saw that he was okay.

"It's Grayson," Jesse told her, and he showed Hanna the message that had just arrived.

Everything's set up. But it's possible word is already out that we have Bull here. Nelda Baker was apparently looking out her window when we drove by her place, and she saw Bull in the cruiser. I didn't spot her at the time or I would have told her to keep quiet. Too late now. The cat's out of the bag because a couple of minutes ago, I got a phone call from Nelda's son asking if it was true, if we had actually arrested Bull.

Hell. Nelda was a notorious gossip and had likely let plenty of people know. Of course, even once the word got back to the militia and their leader, they would still have to come up with their own plan of attack. It was even possible that such an assault wouldn't involve thugs trying to storm the building. They could try to get to Bull by some other means, maybe by finding something or someone they could use to silence him.

Or maybe they'd already gone on the run, believing they were all about to be arrested.

That wasn't a best case scenario as far as Jesse was concerned. If this snake pit went underground, then heaven knew how long it would take to round them all up again. And Jesse doubted they wouldn't take the "go and sin no more" route. Not a chance. They would just set up their illegal operation somewhere else, bide their time and then come after them once they let down their guards. That meant Hanna, Evan, and no one in Jesse's family would be safe.

As much as the idea of a showdown sickened him, he was afraid it was going to come to that. Either now or later. Jesse preferred to save his "later" for getting on with life, and the only way that could happen was for them to neutralize this very large, very dangerous, threat.

"So, the militia's had…what?" Hanna stopped and checked the time. "Over an hour to prepare?"

"Probably," he verified because it had been nearly two hours since Grayson had left.

Even if Nelda had inadvertently informed a militia member with her gossip, it still would have taken some time to get back to the leader. Jesse didn't get the feeling that most members actually knew who the leader was. If so, that would have likely come out with all the arrests that had been made shortly after Hanna's shooting. That would have been powerful bargaining info for anyone looking for a plea deal.

It was a smart move for the leader to act more as a silent partner. A partner who no doubt had raked in big profits from all the illegal activities while keeping his or her identity under wraps.

Jesse sent back a quick Thanks for the update reply to Grayson and looked at Hanna to give her a quick kiss before he got up and started putting his clothes back on. His body was suggesting a whole lot more than a mere kiss though. It was pushing for another round of sex, but he didn't have a second condom. Plus, with the plan to lure out the militia leader now in motion, he needed to be focusing on that.

Hanna groaned softly when she glanced down at her naked body partly covered by a throw Jesse had gotten from a basket on the floor. The groan was likely because her right breast was exposed, giving him more of those "another round" thoughts.

She pulled the cover over it but gave him the quick kiss that he'd been fantasizing about. He wasn't stupid. He knew a kiss wasn't an announcement from her that all was right between them, but it was a good start.

So was the view when she stood to dress.

Her body was still just as amazing as it had been before she'd had Evan, but she frowned when she caught him looking at her. "The C-section scar is still there," she said, tracing the line across her lower abdomen.

Since she seemed to think that would make him remember the terrifying scramble to save Evan's life, Jesse went to her and dropped down low enough to kiss the scar. He didn't even mind the dirty thought he had about giving her some more kisses. He'd just wanted her to know that the scar was all part of who she was. Of what she'd survived.

"You're perfect," he heard himself say, and he winced a little because she could take it as too much, too soon.

She made a sound of disagreement, but it had a light tone to it. "Perfect with stretch marks and a stomach paunch."

Heck, he liked the little paunch, too. Then again, with his body starting to rev, he doubted there was anything about her that would cool him down. But since cooling down was exactly what he had to do, Jesse forced himself to move away from her. *Forced* being the operative word.

He'd already put back on his boxers, jeans and boots just in case he'd had to move in a hurry, but he'd kept the shirt off so he could enjoy the feel of Hanna naked and sleeping against him. He put on his shirt now and watched as she started to do the same with her own clothes.

"Do you think we can trust Bull?" she asked. "I mean do you believe he really intends to help bring down the militia leader?"

That was the million-dollar question, and even

with the amazing sex, it hadn't been that far from his mind. "I think we can trust him to a point. If he's a dirty agent, it seems he's willing to throw the militia under a bus by drawing them out. But then, he had nothing to lose by doing that. Bull's in as much danger, if not more, than the rest of us."

"Yes," she murmured, and she ended the peep show by pulling on her panties and jeans. "The militia leader would want a federal agent dead." She looked at him. "Would they want Shaw dead, too? I mean if he's not the leader, that is."

"They would." Jesse didn't have to give that any thought. "The militia would be looking for payback for anyone who's been involved in tearing the group apart. But I haven't ruled Shaw out yet as a suspect. He could have orchestrated this, and he'd stand a better chance of getting to Bull than some thugs."

She stayed quiet a moment, obviously giving that some thought. "Because Shaw would be able to get into the sheriff's office."

Jesse nodded. "Grayson would keep an eye on him to make sure Shaw doesn't try to execute Bull. Or poison him. But Shaw wouldn't have to do the dirty work himself. Eventually, Bull will have to be transferred to another jail. Or into the custody of the ATF. Shaw could have friends or cohorts who could easily get to Bull and silence him before anything goes to trial."

"And it would be Bull's word against Shaw's if this turns into a federal investigation," she added.

He had to nod again. "I'm betting if Shaw's the

culprit, then he's already hidden or destroyed any proof that Bull could use to point a finger at him."

Of course, it was just as possible there was no evidence to find because Shaw could be innocent. If so, Jesse would owe him an apology, but he had no intention of giving the agent any leeway, or access to Hanna, before he knew one way or another about the agent's involvement or innocence.

Hanna nodded as well. "That leaves Marlene and—" She'd obviously been about to bring up their other suspects, but she stopped when his phone dinged again with a text.

One look at it and Jesse's heart dropped. Because it wasn't Grayson this time. It was Miguel Navarro, the ranch hand who was standing guard.

"'Somebody's here,'" Jesse read aloud from Miguel's text. "'It's one person, on foot, walking up the road toward the house.'"

Hanna made a slight gasp, but he saw her quickly rein in the slam of panic. It could be nothing, but with everything else going on, Jesse was dead certain they wouldn't be that lucky.

Is the person armed? Jesse texted back to Miguel, and he added to Hanna, "Wait here. I'm going to have a look out the front window."

"Be careful," she murmured.

Because she looked many steps beyond the mere worried stage, he took the time to brush a kiss on her mouth before he went to the living room. Jesse had just made it to the window when Miguel responded.

Can't tell, the hand messaged. But it looks like a woman.

Well, that sure as hell didn't put Jesse at ease since two of their suspects were women. Added to that, there could be female members in the militia.

She doesn't look too steady on her feet, Miguel added several moments later. She's staggering like she's drunk. Or hurt.

There was a third option. She could be pretending to be drunk or hurt. A ruse to try to get closer.

Wishing he had binoculars, Jesse peered through the darkness to get a glimpse of their visitor. Of course, the ranch hands and deputy wouldn't let the woman actually approach the house without stopping her to find out what she wanted, but if she was armed, she could start shooting before they even got to her.

Jesse watched as Miguel hurried across the yard to duck behind a tree. He was obviously trying to get in position so he'd have a better angle to keep an eye on their visitor. The moon wasn't cooperating with that though. There was just enough cloud cover to give them very little illumination.

As a cop, Jesse wanted to be out there, to put an end to this himself. But he couldn't risk leaving Hanna and Evan alone.

Jesse's phone dinged again, and this time the text was from the reserve deputy, Roger Norris. It's definitely a woman, he said, adding the ranch hands onto the text. And she looks familiar.

Just as he read that, some of the clouds finally

drifted away, giving Jesse just enough light for him to make out the woman's face.

Hell. She was familiar all right.

Because it was Hanna's mother.

HANNA STAYED IN the doorway of the nursery, trying to hear any bits of info that Jesse was getting about this possible intruder, but she kept her gaze pinned to the baby monitor that she'd picked up. Since her back was to the crib, she couldn't actually see Evan. Might not be able to hear him, either, because her heartbeat was crashing in her ears. So she watched the monitor to make sure he wasn't stirring or waking up.

Every few seconds, she peered out, hoping to get a glimpse of Jesse, but he'd obviously moved to one of the windows out of her line of sight. He was no doubt getting updates from the hands and deputy, and even over her own loud heartbeat, she thought she would have heard any shots that might have been fired. Maybe that meant this was a false alarm, someone who'd maybe broken down and had come to her house looking for help.

Of course, that was wishful thinking, but Hanna held on to that hope until she saw Jesse making his way toward her. One look at his face and she knew something was wrong.

"What happened?" she managed to ask.

He had his gun drawn, but he used his left hand to take hold of her shoulder in what was usually a reassuring gesture. Not much would reassure her at this point though.

"It's your mother," Jesse told her. "She's on foot, and she's coming toward the house."

"On foot?" She shook her head. That didn't make sense. If Isabel had broken down, she had a cell phone, and she could have called. At least she would have if her phone battery hadn't died. Or if she didn't have something else planned.

Like getting close enough to attack.

Hanna still couldn't see Isabel doing something like that, but if she was the militia leader and was desperate, she might be willing to do just about anything. Even get her own hands dirty by launching an attack to silence Jesse and her.

"What are you going to do?" she asked Jesse.

"I don't want to pull any of the deputies away from Grayson's operation, and I think we have enough manpower here to deal with whatever she's trying to bring to your doorstep. My plan right now is to allow her to come closer to the house so I can find out why she's here. I won't let her in," he quickly added. "And the ranch hands and deputy will keep watch to make sure she's alone and hasn't brought *friends* with her."

Good. Because Hanna didn't want those so-called friends getting anywhere near the house so they could start shooting.

"Isabel will want to talk to me," Hanna pointed out. "Does she have her phone with her? If so, she might call when she gets closer."

"Can't tell. She might be drunk. Or hurt." He flexed his grip on her shoulder. "I can't see any blood or anything, but she's staggering."

Jesse didn't ask her if she'd ever known Isabel to get falling-down drunk. She hadn't, as far as she knew, but then she only had six months of memories when it came to her mother. However, Isabel could be hurt despite there not being any signs of blood. If she wasn't the leader of the militia, then she could have been attacked by one of them as a ploy to drag them out of hiding.

"I'm not opening the door to her," Jesse said as if reading her mind. "Not turning off the security system either. But the reserve deputy, Norris, is frisking her right now to make sure she isn't armed. If she doesn't have any kind of weapon and wants to talk to you, I can have her brought onto the porch. You'll be able to speak to her through the window."

Hanna had no problems agreeing to any of that. She had to know why the woman was there, but she didn't want that info if it put anyone at risk.

"Keep the baby monitor with you," he instructed, and she followed him toward the front of the house.

He motioned for her to stay to the side so that she wasn't directly in front of the glass. She did, but Hanna was able to look out into the yard and spot her mother and the deputy. Jesse had been right about her staggering. If the deputy hadn't had hold of her arm, Isabel likely would have fallen.

"I think she might have been drugged," the deputy said in a voice loud enough for them to hear.

Drugged. Oh, mercy. Hanna forced herself to stay put, but her worry skyrocketed. At least, it did until she reminded herself once again that this might all be an act. A potentially deadly one.

"Hanna?" her mother called out. "Please help me. Please."

Jesse muttered some profanity that was laced with as much frustration and worry as Hanna was feeling. "I'll call for an ambulance," he told the deputy, and Jesse did that while Deputy Norris led Isabel onto the porch.

When Isabel passed under the overhead light, Hanna could see that her mother did indeed look dazed. Maybe because she was overdosing on something. Maybe having another stroke. But Hanna didn't know if this was something Isabel had done to herself of if someone had given her drugs. If it was the latter, Hanna wanted to know why.

"The ambulance will be here in about ten minutes," Jesse relayed to Hanna and the deputy.

On the porch, Isabel sank down next to the window, leaned her head against the wooden frame and looked up at Jesse. "I need to see Hanna."

"I'm here," Hanna told her, but she didn't go closer. She stayed back in case a sniper was out there, ready to target her the moment she stepped into view. However, she could still see her mother's face through the glass. "What happened to you?"

Isabel shook her head. "I don't know. I was driving, coming out here, and I got so dizzy." Some of her words were slurred. "Uh, I had to stop…and when I got out to try to get some fresh air, I stumbled and fell." She paused again. "I saw the lights to your house and walked toward them."

"Is it possible someone drugged you?" Jesse came out and asked.

Isabel lifted her head, peering directly at him. Her eyes were definitely unfocused, so that part wasn't an act. "I don't know," she repeated.

"They can do a tox screen on her at the hospital," Hanna heard Jesse murmur. "We can find out what she's taken or been given."

"What were you eating or drinking before you came here?" Jesse pressed, shifting his attention back to Isabel.

Isabel responded with another headshake and more slurred, mumbled words. They were obviously going to have to wait for the effect of the drugs to wear off before they got any answers, but Hanna decided to try one more question.

"Why did you need to see me?" she asked.

Isabel groaned and lifted her head. "Because I'm sorry. So sorry."

Hanna sighed since her mother had obviously come here to rehash her guilt over stirring up Arnie so he'd confront Jesse. "We'll talk about that after you're out of the hospital. I'll call Dr. Warner and let him know what's going on."

The doctor might even have some insight about a possible bad side effect from medication Isabel was taking for her recovery from the stroke.

"You were so mad," Isabel went on, as if talking to herself. "That's the worst argument we've ever had. Even worse than the other ones about Jesse."

That got Hanna's attention. "What do you mean? What argument?"

Isabel closed her eyes. "The one about the money." She was definitely getting groggier, and Hanna didn't think it was a good idea for her to sleep. Not until they knew what had caused this.

"Stay awake, Mother," Hanna snapped, hoping that Isabel would respond to the stern tone. She did. Well, in part. She opened her eyes anyway. "What argument did we have about money?" Hanna demanded.

"The money you found in my account," Isabel muttered as if it were something that Hanna was well aware of.

Hanna glanced at Jesse to see if he knew anything about this, but he only shook his head. This was the first either of them was hearing about it.

"Too much money in there, you said," Isabel rambled on. "You saw my bank statement lying on my desk, and you said it had too much."

Hanna definitely didn't recall any of this either. "Why was the money in your account?" she asked.

"A favor. That's all. That's what I tried to tell you. It was just a favor. But you said it looked like money laundering to you."

Sweet heaven. A single deposit wouldn't have caused her to come to a conclusion like that. There must have been a pattern.

"How much was this favor?" Hanna pressed.

"A hundred thousand, added in increments…" Isabel stopped, groaned, but then shook her head as if trying to clear it. "Added in increments of just under ten thousand."

Hanna couldn't be sure, but she thought those

amounts wouldn't have been reported to the IRS or some other government agency.

"You said you knew the money couldn't be mine because you'd just had a meeting with my accountant about those bad investments I'd made," Isabel continued.

Again, this was news to Hanna. She hadn't known about the investments, the meeting with the accountant or these mystery funds.

In the distance, Hanna heard the sirens and knew the ambulance would be there soon. Once they took Isabel to the hospital, heaven knew how long it'd be before she got to talk to her again. She wanted to clear all of this up now.

"Who put the money in your account?" Hanna went on.

"A friend," Isabel said, her voice barely audible now, and she closed her eyes again.

"What friend?" Jesse and Hanna demanded in unison.

Isabel didn't even try to answer. She'd lost consciousness. Or worse. The deputy must have thought the worst was possible, too, because he touched his fingers to her neck.

"She's alive," he assured them.

Hanna didn't have time for the breath of relief she wanted to take. That's because she heard something that chilled her to the bone.

Somewhere out in the darkness, there was a gunshot.

Chapter Fifteen

Jesse automatically motioned for Hanna to step further back. He didn't want to send her running to the nursery just yet because the shot had sounded far away. It was possibly even a night hunter out in the woods, looking for coyotes but considering what had happened to Isabel, that wasn't likely.

Of course, Isabel could have done this to herself, and that's what Jesse kept in mind while he continued to watch out the window. But if Hanna's mom had told the truth about all that money being in her account, then that was something he could confirm once he took a harder look at her financials. The money certainly hadn't been in there recently because Theo had looked at her accounts, but there was no telling how long ago that argument between Hanna and her mother had happened. Since Isabel hadn't been a suspect in Hanna's shooting, Jesse hadn't dug into her assets.

That would change first chance he got.

Deputy Norris dropped down next to Isabel, obviously shielding her with his own body in case any gunfire came their way, but Jesse listened hard and didn't hear anything else. Well, nothing other than the howl of the ambulance as it got closer to the house.

He took out his phone and texted Dispatch to tell them to have the ambulance hold at the end of the driveway. That way, the EMTs wouldn't be in the line of fire if there were more shots fired. Plus, it would cut down on the risk in case one of the militia thugs had managed to get in the ambulance. Jesse wouldn't put it past them to do something like drug Isabel all so that Hanna and he could be attacked when the EMTs arrived on scene.

"Do you think I came to the ranch that night I was shot to tell you about the argument I had with my mother?" Hanna asked, and the nerves were causing her voice to tremble. Heck, she was trembling, too.

"It's possible," he admitted.

Jesse had questioned himself often as to why she'd come to see him. Yes, she'd had those ultrasound pictures and medical forms with her, but there'd been nothing pressing about them. In fact, he'd later learned that she'd already emailed him the ultrasound photos. He'd also later learned that he could have signed the papers even after she was at the hospital in labor. That had led Jesse to hope that she'd just wanted to see him, to be with the father of her child so they could talk about the upcoming birth. But maybe he had been totally off base.

Instead, it could be connected to Isabel and this money her so-called friend had deposited into her account.

Soon, very soon, he'd also find out exactly who that friend was because it was possible that Isabel would put Arnie, Marlene and even Bull into that friend category. Probably not Agent Shaw, though, unless she'd stayed quiet about knowing the man. That was something else Jesse needed to check.

Because he didn't want to leave Grayson out of the loop, Jesse continued to keep watch and sent him a text.

Isabel showed up here. It appears she's been drugged. We also heard a shot. Not sure if there's an actual threat yet.

He'd just hit Send when Jesse heard Miguel call out. "I spotted someone at the fence near the road."

Maybe this was their shooter, and that was Jesse's cue to take the security up a notch. "It's time for Evan and you to go into the bathroom," Jesse told her.

He looked back at Hanna, trying to silently reassure her that he'd do his best to keep them safe. Jesse wasn't sure he succeeded though. Hanna definitely looked scared out of her mind when she ran toward the nursery.

Hell. He hated that she had to go through this when she'd already been through way too much. Too much that might have been at least partly her own mother's fault. Jesse wasn't sure how Hanna would feel if it turned out he had to arrest Isabel, but if the woman was guilty, she would get what she deserved.

Jesse's phone rang, the sound breaking the silence,

and he saw Grayson's name on the screen. He muttered another, "*Hell*," hoping that something hadn't gone wrong at the sheriff's office.

"I'm on the way out to Hanna's," Grayson said the moment Jesse answered. "I'll be there in a few minutes."

"But what about Bull?" It sure didn't seem like a good idea to shortchange the security there at the jail when Bull might be just as much of a target as Hanna and he were. Added to that, they really needed to catch anyone who might try to go after the man.

"It's covered," Grayson assured him. "I asked Mason to come in to take my place. He'll be able to handle anything that comes up."

Jesse didn't doubt the handling part, but this meant yet another family member was in danger.

"Did you hear any other shots being fired?" Grayson asked.

"No, but I've kept the ambulance on hold just in case."

He hoped like the devil that wasn't a fatal mistake for Isabel, but the deputy was keeping a check of her pulse while he continued looking around the yard.

"Isabel might have been talking out of her head," Jesse went on, "but she described a situation that sounded a lot like her involvement in money laundering. I wasn't able to get the name of who hooked her up with that, but it might be connected to Hanna's shooting."

"I can talk to her once she's at the hospital. I'll follow the ambulance there and put her under guard."

Good, because someone might be out to kill her, too. "Let me text the ambulance driver to come on up and get her," Jesse said, getting ready to do that.

But then he heard the crack of gunfire.

It wasn't just one shot this time but three in a row, and he was darn sure it had come from the vicinity of the bottom of the driveway. Right where the ambulance was parked.

"I see the shooter," one of the ranch hands yelled. "Looks like it's a guy on the side of the road with a rifle."

Jesse hissed out a breath because that's exactly where Grayson was heading. "Stay back," Jesse warned him just as he heard the squeal of brakes. "There's an active shooter in the area."

"Yeah," Grayson verified. "He's shooting at me."

That sent his pulse racing so it was thick and throbbing in his head. The SOB was trying to kill Grayson. Or create some kind of distraction. Either way, it wasn't a good situation to have Grayson under fire.

"Do you have any reserves you can call in?" Jesse asked.

"No cops available, but I'll call for some more of the ranch hands. Not sure how long it'll take them to get here, but I'll keep you posted. Just focus on keeping Hanna and Evan safe."

He would. They came first, but he had another problem to deal with.

"I'm going to have to get Isabel inside," Jesse muttered.

It was a risk. Anything he did at this point would

be. But he couldn't leave Deputy Norris and her outside where they'd both be easy targets. Of course, the ranch hands were out there, as well, but they could take cover. Norris and Isabel couldn't do that, and with the porch light shining down on them, gunmen wouldn't have any trouble spotting them.

"Watch your back," Grayson advised him, and it appeared he was ready to end the call when Jesse heard him snarl. "Agent Shaw. What the heck is he doing out here?"

"Shaw's there? Is he the shooter?" Jesse couldn't ask fast enough.

"Yeah, he's by the fence across the road from Hanna's." There was the sound of more gunfire. "But he's not the one firing at me."

It didn't mean, though, that Shaw wasn't calling the shots—literally. The gunmen could be thugs acting on his orders.

"The bullets are slamming into the windshield of the cruiser," Grayson added a heart-stopping moment later. "The glass is holding, but I'm not sure for how long. I'm going to try to back up and get to the ranch trail just up the road. I can use it to make my way to Hanna's."

Jesse definitely didn't like the idea of Grayson being on an isolated trail where gunmen could be lying in wait for him, but he didn't want him just sitting there while someone tried to kill him.

"Be careful," Jesse told him, knowing that he wouldn't be able to talk Grayson into just backing off out of the line of fire and waiting.

Part of Jesse didn't want to talk him into it either. Because if Grayson could get to the house, that meant there'd be one extra lawman to make sure these gunmen didn't get anywhere near Hanna and Evan.

Grayson ended the call, but Jesse didn't go to the door. He took a second to try to call Shaw, and it surprised him when the agent answered on the first ring.

"Why the hell are you here?" Jesse demanded.

"I followed Isabel." Shaw hadn't hesitated, but he sounded out of breath. "Don't trust her. I think she's involved with the militia."

For once, Jesse agreed with the agent on both counts. He had no intention of getting into the possibility of money laundering though. Not with Grayson under fire.

"Who's shooting at the cruiser?" Jesse snapped.

"Some guy with a rifle. And, no, I don't know who it is, and it isn't someone working for me. I'm not dirty, and I'm trying to get into position to take out the shooter."

Jesse wished he could be sure of that because it would mean they had extra backup on scene. "Just be careful that no shots come near the house," Jesse warned him.

He didn't wait to hear Shaw's response because time might be running out for Isabel and Deputy Norris, so Jesse ended the call and turned to go to the door.

The sound stopped him.

Not gunfire. But one of the ranch hands yelling.

Then, coughing. Seconds later, Jesse saw the white fog sliding across the yard toward the house.

"Tear gas," Norris managed to say though he, too, started coughing. "We need to get inside *now*."

HANNA'S HEART WAS in her throat, and her muscles tightened with the sound of each and every bullet that was being fired. Sweet heaven, there was a gunfight going on. One that could get Jesse, her mother and everyone helping them killed.

She pressed Evan closer to her, not to soothe him. He was asleep. She was the one who needed soothing, and she wished she knew what was going on. It didn't seem as if the bullets were being fired near the house, so maybe that meant the ranch hands and Deputy Norris were holding off attackers. If so, she prayed they succeeded. Prayed, too, they all got out of this alive.

She thought of her mother, drugged and dazed on the porch, and she added a prayer that Isabel wasn't a major player in all of this. Money laundering was bad enough. So was withholding the truth about what had gone on right before Arnie had shot her. But if Isabel's actions had caused the danger, then Hanna wanted her to pay and pay hard.

Hanna heard one of the ranch hands shouting, and she made out the words. *Tear gas.* Oh, mercy. That caused her heart to skip a beat or two. Because if their attackers had set off tear gas, he or she might have done it so they could get Jesse, Evan and her out of the house.

"It's me," someone said at the door.

Jesse.

The relief washed over her. He was alive, and she hurried out of the bathtub so she could unlock the door for him. He wasn't hurt. That was the first thing she made sure of, but every bit of his expression and body language told her they were in deep trouble.

"How bad is it?" she asked.

"Grayson's on the way," he said, and she knew he was trying to give her the good news first. "Someone set off tear gas canisters at the end of the driveway, and the ranch hands had to scatter."

In other words, they probably wouldn't be able to hold off any gunmen making their way to the house.

"I got your mother and Deputy Norris inside," Jesse continued. "He's watching her to make sure she doesn't try anything."

Anything—as in try to kill them to make sure they stayed silent about her involvement with the militia.

"The house is locked up, and I've reset the security system. No one will get in without us knowing about it. I'm also staying here with Evan and you," he assured her. "The tear gas will clear soon—" He stopped when someone fired a shot.

Not on the road from the sound of it. This was nearby.

Maybe even in the yard.

Hanna tried not to let the fear take over. She couldn't panic because Jesse didn't have time to try to bring her out of a full-scale attack. But her heart was pounding and her breath was already going thin.

Jesse pulled the bathroom door shut and he locked it. "Get back in the tub," he instructed.

Just hearing Jesse's voice helped some even though what he was saying meant the danger was imminent. Still, she used the sound of his voice to start steadying herself. Hanna also kept her attention on Evan's peaceful, sleeping face, which was better than any of the grounding exercises the therapist had taught her. She had to stay in control for the sake of her baby.

There were no windows in the bathroom, and the only illumination came from a cheery turtle night-light plugged into the outlet on the vanity. It was enough light, though, for her to see Jesse. He stayed at the door, no doubt ready to defend them if anyone came through. And he would defend them. Hanna was certain of that. However, she was equally certain that Jesse could die if it came down to it.

As if he sensed what she was thinking, Jesse looked back at her, their gazes connecting. He was trying to reassure her again. But that reassurance vanished when the night-light went out, plunging them into total darkness.

Seconds later, the security alarm went off, the sound blaring and echoing through the house.

Evan jolted and started to cry, though Hanna could barely hear him over the noise. She pulled him to her, tried to soothe him, and once again had to battle her own panic.

Because it was possible the gunmen were in the house.

That was the thought that kept repeating in her

head. A thought that was throbbing with her too fast heartbeat and her racing breath. Just when she thought she couldn't take any more, the alarms stopped, and the room went deadly silent. That's when she realized Evan had stopped crying, but he was whimpering as if trying to lull himself back to sleep.

"I had to use the app to turn off the security," Jesse whispered to her. "I have to be able to hear them if they come this way."

She didn't have to ask what he meant by *them*. The gunmen. Maybe even the militia leader. Yes, Jesse would definitely need to know if they were trying to get into the bathroom. But she didn't hear anything like that.

No running footsteps.

No gunfire.

She tried not to assume a worst case scenario: that the ranch hands outside the house had all been killed. But it was possible.

"They got her," a man shouted. He was coughing.

"That was Deputy Norris," Jesse muttered.

So, not one of the gunmen, and Hanna heard those running footsteps she'd been listening for. Steps in the hall coming toward the nursery.

Jesse turned on the flashlight app on his phone and opened the bathroom door. "Someone took Isabel?" he called out.

"Yeah," the deputy verified, causing Hanna's heart to pound even harder. He continued to cough. "Someone broke through the front door and threw in more tear gas. I couldn't see, but whoever it was, bashed me on the head and took her. I'm sorry," he added with a groan. "They took her."

Even though Hanna wasn't sure of her mother's innocence, that still caused her fear to soar. Isabel could be in the hands of killers right now.

"Who took her?" Jesse pressed.

"Couldn't tell. The person had on a gas mask and was wearing bulky clothes."

So it could have been anyone. Including Shaw or Marlene. Or someone one of them had hired to do it.

"How bad are you hurt?" Jesse asked the deputy.

"Uh, I think I'm okay," Norris answered, but he didn't sound okay at all. He was still coughing. "You should stay put. The tear gas is clearing up some, but it's still hard to breathe out here."

Jesse cursed under his breath. "Stay here. I'll let Norris in here and then try to contact the ranch hands."

Hanna nodded and fumbled to get her phone from her jeans' pocket so that she could turn on the flashlight, too. It helped because she could see Evan's face. Could see that he'd fallen back to sleep. That was something at least. It would have skyrocketed her stress if he'd been terrified and sobbing.

Several seconds later, Jesse rushed back into the bathroom, and he had Norris in tow. There was blood on the side of the deputy's head and he did indeed look as dazed as he'd sounded.

"I'm so sorry about your mother," Norris told her.

She nodded and watched as Jesse and the deputy positioned themselves on either side of the bathroom door. They didn't shut and lock it, probably since this way they'd have a clear line of sight of anyone trying to come into the nursery.

Because the room was quiet now, she heard Jesse's phone vibrate, a setting he'd likely used so it wouldn't alert anyone to their position in the house.

"It's Grayson," he told her in a whisper.

Even though Jesse hadn't put the call on speaker, she could still hear Grayson when he spoke. "What's your status?" Grayson asked.

"Not good," Jesse replied. "Someone cut the power and used tear gas to get into the house and take Isabel. The person bashed Norris on the head. I think he's all right," he added, giving the deputy a glance, "and we're holding up in the nursery bathroom."

She wasn't able to hear what Grayson said next, but she thought he cursed.

"What's your status?" Jesse repeated to Grayson.

"I'm threading my way through this trail to Hanna's. So far, no gunmen in sight. When I get to the house, I'll drive straight to the porch and get as close to the door as possible. We can get Hanna and Evan into the cruiser and take them to the ranch. Then, I can look for Isabel."

Hanna wanted all of those things to happen. She didn't want to stay here with Evan. But going outside could be just as dangerous as staying put.

"I'll be there in about five minutes," Grayson said before he ended the call.

Five minutes would no doubt seem like an eternity, but Jesse and Norris continued to stand guard at the door.

"I'll try to get one of the ranch hands to respond," Jesse explained when he pressed in a number.

She heard the rings and, with each one, the sense of dread inside her grew. Finally, though, someone answered.

But it wasn't good news.

"We can't get back to the house," the hand choked out between coughs. "Someone keeps shooting tear gas canisters at us."

Oh, mercy. That had to be so someone could get inside.

"Are you hurt?" Jesse pressed.

"No. Just my eyes and nose stinging like fire from the tear gas. I can't see, Jesse. I can't be sure if somebody's not trying to get in."

More dread washed over her, and it got worse when she heard the voice. Not the ranch hand out in the yard. This had come from inside the house.

"Hanna," the woman shouted.

Isabel.

Hanna jerked in a hard breath. She couldn't be sure, but it sounded as if her mother was in the hall, right outside the nursery.

"Hanna," Isabel repeated, and then added, "Jesse. Please you have to help me."

Chapter Sixteen

Jesse didn't move. He sure as hell didn't go rushing out into the hall to help Isabel, despite her plea.

Because that plea could all be just a ruse to draw him out so Isabel could shoot him.

He didn't know for sure what her motive might be for wanting him dead, but he couldn't take the chance. Not when that would leave Hanna and Evan even more vulnerable than they already were. Later, he'd kick himself for letting things come to this point. But for now, he just kept watch and hoped that a lot of things went right for them. They were going to need some luck to get through this.

"Text Grayson," Jesse whispered to Deputy Norris. "Let him know that Isabel is in the house."

Jesse didn't want to risk taking his attention off the nursery door even for a second to send that message, but he also didn't want Grayson walking in where he could be shot.

"Are you alone, Isabel?" Jesse called out.

With the sound of his voice, Isabel would be able to pinpoint his location, but since she was Hanna's mother, the woman would have almost certainly known where they'd be.

Isabel coughed, maybe from the remnants of the tear gas. Or because she wanted them to believe she was affected by it. It was just as possible that she'd gotten access to a gas mask, given to her by one of the militia goons, and that she'd just now removed the mask so the coughing would make her appeal for help seem more genuine.

"No," Isabel said, her voice barely audible because of the coughing. "I—" She cut off whatever she'd been about to add.

Or had been cut off.

Jesse heard a sound, a sort of swooshing gasp that a person might make if they'd just been punched in the stomach and the breath had been knocked out of them. Again, that could be faked, but the next sounds he heard were the real deal.

Footsteps.

Someone was definitely in the hall.

He hadn't locked the door to the nursery because he'd figured it wouldn't do any good. If the gunmen had gotten that far, they would have just broken it down, and the flying wood might have prevented Jesse from seeing them clearly. This way, he could watch and wait for them to come in, and when they did, he could put an end to their miserable lives.

Jesse didn't relish the idea of shooting anyone, especially didn't want to kill even when the other person was a killer, but he had no intentions of letting them continue to wreak this deadly havoc.

Of course, a gunfight this close to Evan and Hanna could turn out the worst kind of bad. The bathtub gave them some protection. Some. And this was where luck came in. Maybe it would be enough to keep them both out of the path of any bullets that were fired.

"Grayson will come the rest of the way on foot," Norris whispered after he'd gotten a response to his text. "He'll try to sneak into the house and take Isabel and anyone who's with her from behind."

Hell, there were a dozen things that could go wrong with that plan. The gunmen could spot Grayson and shoot him. He might even be hit with friendly fire if the ranch hands mistook him for the militia. Added to that, Agent Shaw was still out there somewhere, and there was no telling what his intentions were. But Jesse reminded himself that Grayson was as smart a lawman as they came. He'd be careful because he knew how high the stakes were.

"I, uh, need you to come out so we can talk," Isabel finally said.

Her voice was strained, but he couldn't tell if it was real or put on.

"Not a chance," Jesse responded. "Are you alone?" he repeated.

The woman didn't make that hard gasp this time, but she also didn't respond to Jesse's question. However, because Jesse was listening carefully, he heard more of those footsteps. Maybe two sets, indicating that someone was indeed with her, but he couldn't be sure.

He glanced back at Hanna and Evan, the light from

her phone casting an eerie shadow on her face. He saw the worry. And the fear. But he also saw something else. Her determination to keep their son safe. She shifted in the tub, lying Evan down so she could hover over him.

Shield him with her body.

Putting herself in a position in case she had to fight.

Jesse hated she had to take a risk like that, but it was necessary. They were parents, and their child came first. He hadn't needed a reminder like that to know just how much he loved Evan.

Hanna, too.

Maybe, just maybe he'd get the chance to tell both of them that. But for that to happen, he had to put an end to the threat.

His gaze slashed back to the door when he heard the sound of the knob moving. Possibly Isabel, but it was more likely a gunman. Someone who'd be ready to start firing at first chance.

Jesse turned off his flashlight, slipped his phone back in his pocket, and took aim. Waiting, while every nerve and muscle in his body went on full alert.

"Isabel?" Jesse called out when the door opened just a fraction.

"Yes—" Again, the woman was cut off or merely stopped to make it sound that way. There were a couple of heart-stopping seconds before she finally added, "Don't shoot me."

"Don't give me a reason to shoot you," Jesse countered.

Isabel made a strangled sound, one that might have been terror, and the door opened even wider. Jesse cursed the darkness because his eyes were still adjusting, and he could only see the outline of a person. He wasn't sure if it was Isabel or someone else. But what he didn't spot was a weapon.

"I'm sorry," Isabel said.

Like her coughs and other sounds, it seemed genuine. *Seemed.* "For what?" Jesse demanded. He adjusted his aim as the door fully opened and the woman stepped closer. Not actually into the room though. Isabel stayed in the doorway.

And she wasn't alone.

There was someone standing behind her. And this time when he looked, Jesse did see a weapon.

It was aimed at Isabel's head.

Jesse braced for the gut-slam of adrenaline, and it came. He did a quick assessment of the situation and realized that even if Isabel was truly in danger, he didn't have a clean shot to take out the person who could be holding her at gunpoint.

A person who could be a man or woman.

Whoever it was, they weren't that much taller than Isabel, which didn't rule out either Shaw or Marlene. Of course, the person could also be stooping down to try to disguise his or her height, and he or she was wearing what appeared to be a gas mask.

"I'm supposed to tell you that you need to come with me," Isabel said, her voice shaking.

She was shaking, too. Jesse could see that now that his eyes had finally adjusted, and he thought she was still feeling the effects of whatever drug she'd taken or been given.

"You and Hanna are supposed to come out," Isabel added when her captor dug the gun harder into the side of her head. She made another sob. "The baby can stay here where he'll be safe."

"Safe," Jesse snapped. "With armed men shooting bullets and tear gas. He woke up crying when the security alarm went off. Terrified and crying." In the grand scheme of things, that probably wouldn't seem like a big deal to some people.

Including a would-be killer.

But Jesse's comment seemed to hit the mark with Isabel. Evan's grandmother. She let out a hoarse sob. She swung as if to punch the person holding her, but that didn't work. Her captor merely tightened the grip around Isabel's neck.

Jesse got the motherlode of flashbacks. To the night Hanna had been shot. It'd been dark then, too, and Arnie had held her in an almost identical pose with the gun to her head. He hadn't had a clear shot then. Hadn't been able to do anything while Arnie had dragged Hanna into the trees and shot her.

Hanna was no doubt hearing all of this, and he prayed she wasn't on the verge of a panic attack. Prayed that they could do enough to get through this. But it had to cut her to the bone to know that her mother was in danger. Or that Isabel was the cause of all of this.

"Grayson's here," Norris whispered, yanking Jesse out of those nightmarish images. "He's in the house."

A different kind of image came. And it played out right in front of him. The image of Grayson being gunned down.

Jesse heard the sound of Grayson's footsteps. Obviously, so did the man or woman holding Isabel.

In a quick move, the person turned and fired a shot. Not in Grayson's direction though.

The shot came directly toward Jesse.

THE SOUND OF the gunshot was deafening. And Hanna's first thought was Jesse. Had he been shot?

She forced herself to look and saw Jesse lurch to the side. For a split second, it seemed as if the worst had happened. But Jesse didn't fall. Deputy Norris did, and Jesse had moved to catch him.

Both of them went to the floor with Jesse pulling the deputy against the wall and away from the door. Even in the darkness, Hanna could see the blood spread across the sleeve of his shirt. He'd been hit in his right arm.

Norris grunted in pain and he clamped his hand over the wound to stop the flow of blood. What he almost certainly wouldn't be able to do was return fire if it came down to that.

And it did.

Someone fired a second shot, and it tore through a chunk of the doorjamb. Muttering some profanity, Jesse shifted, practically shoving Norris behind him, and he took aim at the shooter. He didn't fire. Maybe because he didn't have a clear shot, but the shooter didn't pull the trigger again either.

Hanna figured that wasn't going to last.

Grayson was somewhere in the house, but it was possible he couldn't move closer without getting shot or risking Isabel being killed. Hanna hadn't actually seen her mother, but she'd heard enough of her conversation with Jesse to know that she was being held at gunpoint. Maybe willingly. Maybe not.

"Get in the tub with the baby," Hanna told Norris. "Jesse needs backup."

Jesse was already trying to nix that idea before she finished, but he couldn't actually argue with her because he had to keep his focus on Isabel and the person who'd fired those shots.

Norris was still bleeding, still clearly in a lot of pain, but he made it to the tub and did as she had asked, acting as a human shield for Evan. Hanna took his gun and scrambled to the other side of the door, across from Jesse.

"You shouldn't be here," Jesse snarled. "Do you even remember how to fire a gun?"

She did, though she hadn't known that until that very second. She'd taken shooting lessons after she'd moved to this current house because she'd wanted to be able to scare off coyotes. The stakes were much higher now, and Hanna knew in her gut that she wouldn't miss.

"Hanna," her mother said. It was possible Isabel had gotten a glimpse of her when she'd traded places with Norris.

Hanna made a quick glance around the jamb and saw her mother. And the person behind her. The person wasn't looking at Jesse or her, though, but rather toward the living room. He or she gave Isabel a hard squeeze before whispering something in her ear.

"Grayson," Isabel called out a moment later, "if you want Jesse and Hanna to live, then you need to leave."

She didn't hear Grayson respond, but Hanna knew he wouldn't leave. But maybe he'd be able to distract Isabel's captor. Or maybe Isabel would drop down. Anything to give one of them a shot.

Deputy Norris's phone was on the floor and the screen lit up with a text. From Grayson. Two words flashed on the screen.

It's Marlene.

Hanna lifted the phone to show to Jesse, and he shook his head in disgust. Hanna felt the disgust, too, but there was also some relief because maybe this meant her mother hadn't actually been capable of killing anyone.

"It's over, Marlene," Jesse called out.

Silence, but Hanna did see the woman stiffen, and when she cursed and Hanna heard her voice, she knew Grayson had been right.

"You've got a choice here, Jesse," Marlene sniped as she yanked off the gas mask she'd been wearing. "I'll leave, and you'll never see or hear from me again. Just let me walk out of here and Hanna and your son stay safe."

Hanna didn't believe that for a second, and she was sure Jesse didn't either. With Marlene's resources, if she escaped, she'd be back eventually. Or send her hired thugs to finish them off.

"Let you walk out of here with a hostage?" Jesse countered. "I don't think so."

Marlene huffed. "I'll let Isabel go, too, just as soon as I'm away from the house. Just as I'm sure you and yours won't gun me down."

"Let her take me," Isabel insisted. She was crying now, and her breath was coming out in short, hiccupping sobs. "That way, she won't be anywhere near Evan or Hanna."

That made up for some of the anger Hanna felt for her mother, but it was an offer that Hanna knew Marlene would take. She couldn't afford not to. Without a hostage, she stood no chance of getting away.

Well, maybe she didn't.

There was probably at least one of her men near the driveway. Either that or Marlene had managed to fire all those shots and set off those gas canisters herself.

"Your militia buddies aren't going to save you," Jesse said while he made a subtle shift in his position. He was still looking for an opening to take a shot. "And we have enough proof to put you away for a long, long time."

"You have no proof," she snapped.

"You were in the trees the night Arnie shot me," Hanna threw out there. Partly a bluff. "You also talked my mother into helping you by depositing dirty money into her account."

Marlene didn't deny any of that, but she was shuffling around, her gaze volleying toward the living room. She was trapped and getting desperate. Hanna doubted she'd just shoot Isabel, but that gun could go off.

"This shouldn't be happening," Marlene yelled. "Why couldn't you just have died when Arnie shot you? Then, I wouldn't have had to worry about what you did or didn't remember, about what you did or didn't see." Marlene wailed and cursed some vile words.

Hanna wanted to ask what it was she could have seen or heard, but Jesse spoke first, and he went with a different angle.

"How long have you known your brother was an ATF agent?" Jesse asked. "One who came back into your life with the sole purpose of bringing down a militia you were running."

"When the hell do you think I found out?" the woman snapped. "It was the night Arnie went off the deep end. The idiot. I tried to calm him down, tried to tell him that I'd deal with it if you arrested him, but he wouldn't hear of it. He had to go out there and mess everything up."

The coldness in the woman's words sickened Hanna. Marlene didn't care one bit that Arnie had nearly killed her and her baby. She only cared about Arnie bringing heat to the militia.

Her militia.

"So, what happened?" Jesse pressed. "You went to the ranch, hoping to intercept Arnie, and you witnessed the shooting. Then, you heard Bull tell Hanna he was a deep cover agent."

"My own brother," Marlene railed, verifying what Jesse had just suggested. "I was shocked, stunned.

Horrified. And that's the only reason I didn't kill him then and there. I waited a heartbeat too long, and then you and your cousin arrived on scene. I couldn't kill all of you because I didn't know how many other Rylands and ranch hands were running to the rescue."

"That's why you stayed hidden," Jesse finished for her. "But then you started worrying about what else Bull might have told Hanna."

"Damn right I was worried. I didn't know if Bull had connected me to the Brotherhood or not. I knew I'd have to keep a watch on Hanna. As long as she didn't remember what happened, she wasn't a threat, but Isabel said your memory was starting to come back."

And there it was.

Finally, the truth.

But it was also what Marlene had obviously hoped to be her parting words to them because she started to back away with Isabel in tow. She muttered something, not to any of them, but into what Hanna thought might be a communicator clipped to her collar.

"I'm on the move," Marlene told whoever was on the other end of the device. "Help me get out of here."

Jesse moved fast, and he took aim. Not at Marlene but at the wall just over her head. He fired, the sound of the gunshot blasting through the house.

On a howl of outrage, Marlene whirled around to aim at Jesse just as another shot slammed into the wall. That one had no doubt come from Grayson. Marlene turned, dragging Isabel tighter against her. Or rather, trying to do that, but Isabel started fighting her.

Hanna got hit with the flashbacks of her own attack, but she didn't give in to them. She just kept the gun ready in case she was the one who got the right shot.

Screaming and cursing, Marlene lost her grip on Isabel, who was struggling hard to get away. The moment Isabel finally managed to drop down to the floor, Hanna was ready to pull the trigger.

But Jesse beat her to it.

He went for the kill shot to the head, probably because he couldn't risk a wounded Marlene getting the chance to return fire. The woman froze, her startled gaze locking with Hanna's for just a split second before the life drained from her eyes. She fell, crumpling into a heap on the floor.

Hanna froze, too, but it was from the relief that was already washing over her. It didn't last though. The fear and worry returned with a vengeance when Grayson rushed into view. He glanced around, helping Isabel to her feet while he all but carried her into the bathroom. It was probably overkill, but he went ahead and frisked Isabel to make sure she wasn't armed.

She wasn't.

Grayson's forehead bunched up when he spotted Norris. "The ambulance is nearby, and I'll give the EMTs the go ahead to come here." He shifted toward Jesse. "You stay here and make sure no one gets in the house. We need to round up every last one of her henchmen. Because they're still out there, and they no doubt have orders to kill."

Chapter Seventeen

Orders to kill.

Jesse had no doubts whatsoever about that, but he hated that the reminder had put a fresh layer of fear all over Hanna's face. Not Evan's though. Jesse didn't know how the baby had managed it, but he'd fallen back asleep despite the hell and chaos going on around him.

"How much backup do you have?" Jesse asked Grayson.

"Enough. Some deputies just arrived, and they've already started looking. The ranch hands, too. Stay here," he repeated. "I'll lock the front doors, and you turn on the security system. Hold on to that a little while longer," Grayson added when he tipped his head to the gun Hanna was holding.

Jesse hated to put that kind of burden on her, but another thing was for certain—she would do what she had to. Despite the trauma she'd been through, no way would Hanna just sit back while they were still in danger.

Grayson hurried out, and once Jesse heard him lock up, he rearmed the security system. Of course, one of the militia thugs could have sneaked in by now, so that's why Jesse stood by the door and kept watch. Hanna did the same across from him.

"I'm so sorry," Isabel muttered in a soft sob, and she kept repeating it.

"Mother, you need to get in the tub with the baby," Hanna told her.

Maybe that was just to get Isabel to focus on something other than her regret, but it seemed to work. The woman paused for just a moment before she swiped at her tears, blinked away some more of them and maneuvered into the small space next to Evan. When she saw the blood on Norris's arm, Isabel even grabbed a towel off the bar and wrapped it around the wound.

Good. That would help Norris, and giving Isabel something to do might keep her from crying. She had a right to start sobbing after nearly being killed, but Jesse preferred she put that guilt on hold.

"My mother will go to jail, won't she?" Hanna asked him in a whisper. "Because of the money laundering."

Jesse didn't lie to her. "It's possible. She might be able to work out some kind of plea deal and get away with parole and community service."

She nodded. "I don't think she has anything to do with the attacks."

"No," Jesse agreed. He was mentally piecing it together, and he could see this all went back to Marlene. Once they'd had a chance to go through all her financials, they might be able to figure out just how long she'd been involved in the tangle of illegal activities.

A tangle that he wished Bull had uncovered before Hanna had been shot.

But Bull and Isabel weren't the only ones at fault here.

"Don't," he heard Hanna say, and she surprised him when she leaned over and brushed a kiss on his mouth. "I know what's going on in your head right now. You're thinking if you'd arrested Arnie sooner, then none of the rest of this would have happened."

"I was thinking it because it's true," he pointed out.

Thanks to the flashlight app on their phones, the room was lit enough now that he had no trouble seeing her fierce expression. "But maybe something worse would have gone down if you had managed to arrest Arnie. Something like his arrest could have triggered Marlene to order hits on all of you. On us," she amended. "And we wouldn't have known to watch out for her."

Jesse knew that was possible, but it was still hard for him to clear his conscience. Hanna must have read his mind on that, as well, because she kissed him again. And this time it had a kick of heat despite everything else that was going on.

Isabel made a soft sound. Not a gasp, but one look at her and it was obvious she'd seen that kiss.

"Not a word from you on this," Hanna warned her. "I'm not going to let your bad blood with Jesse's family bleed onto me again. Understand?"

Jesse expected Isabel to have a say about that. She always had when it came to her daughter being involved with a Ryland, but maybe the night had changed her. Or at least made her see that bad blood could be forgiven.

So could his guilt over not having done more to stop Hanna from being shot.

Jesse figured it wasn't over and done. Ditto for Isabel's dislike of him, but this felt like a start. He would take it.

When Norris groaned, Jesse glanced over at him to see how he was doing. There didn't seem to be any fresh blood on the towel Isabel had used, so that was good news. Maybe it wouldn't be long before the ambulance would be able to get to the house and take both Isabel and him to the hospital. And that prompted Jesse to ask Hanna's mom some questions.

"Did Marlene drug you?" he asked.

Isabel nodded. "She must have put something in my coffee. She came over to talk and claimed she was worried about what was going on with Hanna and these attacks." Some anger flashed through her eyes. "She wasn't worried. She drugged me and then kept telling me how I had to drive out here and demand that Hanna and Evan come back to my estate." She stopped, swallowed hard. "Marlene wanted me to be a distraction so she could get those militia members onto the grounds."

Yeah, that was Jesse's take in it, too. Unfortunately, it had worked, and whoever had fired at Grayson on the road had added to the distraction and prevented Grayson from getting to the house to help them.

"I'm not sure how Marlene managed to cut the

power to the house," Jesse muttered, "but it's possible somebody in the militia knew how to do that."

Knew, too, how to get their hands on the tear gas canisters they'd used to scatter the ranch hands. Of course, a group who dealt in illegal weapons and drugs likely wouldn't have had trouble getting supplies like that.

"The CSIs will have to process the house," Hanna said, drawing his attention back to her.

Not that his attention had strayed too far. Along with keeping watch, Jesse made frequent glances at Hanna and Evan to make sure they were okay. They were, but he probably wouldn't be certain of that until he could hold them in his arms. He considered doing that now, but he knew it should wait.

"They will," he agreed. And he hated that her home would be off limits to her for a while. Maybe forever. He didn't know if she'd ever feel safe here after what'd happened tonight.

"Evan and I can go to your place?" Hanna asked.

Isabel opened her mouth, probably to say they could come to her estate, but the look Hanna gave her silenced the woman.

"Of course," Jesse assured her, and while that wasn't a hug, it gave him a whole lot of comfort. Neither Hanna nor Evan had ever stayed the night at his house, and it would be great to have them there.

Not just temporarily, either.

Jesse thought back to those terrifying moments when they had realized they were under attack. The moment when he'd realized just how much he loved her. And he did. That wasn't a false feeling created by the adrenaline. He loved both Evan and her, but he wouldn't lay that all on her now. Best to give her some time to come down from what she had gone through.

"I'm in love with you," Hanna said.

When Jesse heard the words, at first he thought he'd said them, that he had blurted it out, after all. But he looked up and realized Hanna had spoken them.

To him.

"You don't have to do anything about it," she added, making a gesture as if waving that off.

Jesse would have definitely done something if, at that exact moment, his phone hadn't vibrated with a call from Grayson. Talk about bad timing. But in this case, it was warranted because it was good news.

"We got them," Grayson immediately said. "Rounded them all up. I'm at the front door, so I need you to let me in."

Jesse hurried to the front to do just that, but he didn't linger for Grayson to fill him in. He went back to the bathroom. Outside, he heard the ambulance, another good sign.

Grayson came to the bathroom door and looked in at them, obviously checking to make sure everyone was okay. They were, but they probably showed every bit of the fierce battle they'd just fought.

"You're sure you got all of the thugs?" Hanna asked.

Grayson nodded. "Shaw helped. So did the ranch hands once the tear gas had cleared. There were three gunmen. One clammed up, but the other two decided they wanted to confess to any and everything. They independently told us that Marlene had brought three of them with her."

Three. Not an army exactly, but they clearly had managed to do a lot of damage. They could have done more.

"We can wait in here until the EMTs arrive," Grayson went on, "and then I can take you to wherever you need to go in the cruiser."

"The ranch," Jesse and Hanna said at the same time.

Grayson's only reactions were a lifted eyebrow and brief smile, but it was obvious he approved. "It shouldn't take long before I can get you there. Theo and Ava are taking the three thugs to jail now. Obviously, we won't hold them with Bull. We'll be releasing him."

Jesse was okay with that even if he couldn't do the whole forgive-and-forget deal for Bull not being able to stop Arnie from shooting Hanna. But that wasn't a reason for him to stay behind bars. If Bull had been involved in anything illegal, Marlene would have ratted him out since it was obvious she hated her brother for being a deep cover agent.

"So, there's no indications that Shaw was dirty?" Hanna asked Grayson.

"None, and since he jumped right in to help us tonight, I'm inclined to believe he's clean. The ATF will have the final say on that though. I'm sure their internal affairs will pick through everything and make sure both Bull and Shaw haven't bent or flat-out broken the law."

Yeah, that IA investigation would be a given in

a situation like this. The ATF would probably also fully take over dismantling the militia, and that was a chore that Jesse knew Grayson would gladly hand over to them.

"Thank you," Isabel said, and she glanced at Grayson, Jesse and then Hanna. "If you hadn't fired those shots, I might not have been able to get away from Marlene. How did you even know it was her?" she added to Grayson.

"I heard her when she whispered something to one of those thugs through her lapel communicator and I recognized her voice."

Jesse, too, had heard those whispers, but he hadn't been close enough to ID Marlene.

"I wonder why Marlene decided to come here and try to do her own dirty work." Hanna threw it out there.

"Maybe because she was fed up with her men failing," Jesse said. "Or maybe she wanted to personally settle this score."

Since Marlene was dead, they might never know. Well, unless she'd shared her plan with the three men they now had in custody.

When the EMTs came rushing into the nursery, Hanna handed Deputy Norris back his gun, and she picked up Evan from the tub. She also pressed a kiss to Isabel's cheek. A gesture that brought tears to the woman's eyes.

"I'll see you soon," Hanna told her mother and she, while cuddling Evan close to her, followed Jesse into the nursery.

"Let me bring the cruiser to the front, and we can

go," Grayson explained, heading out to leave Hanna, Evan and him alone.

Jesse took full advantage of that lull to do what he'd been needing to do. He gathered both Evan and Hanna into his arms, and he brushed a kiss on the top of Evan's head. The boy could certainly sleep because he didn't even budge.

Hanna budged though. In a way. She smiled when he kissed her not on her head but on the mouth. Jesse had intended to leave it at just that. Something short and sweet, a little celebration that they'd survived in one piece.

He went to move back, but Hanna took hold of Jesse's chin and pulled him to her. There was nothing short or sweet about the kiss she gave him. It was long, deep and filled with the emotion he could practically taste.

"You said something about being in love with me," he reminded her.

"I am." There was emotion in her voice, and lots and lots of heat.

"Good," Jesse said, "because I'm in love with you, too." That led to another kiss. One with way too much heat considering they were standing in the nursery just a few feet away from EMTs, Isabel and the wounded deputy.

Jesse put the heat on pause, knowing he could fire it right up as soon as he had Hanna at his place.

She looked up at him and ran her thumb over his jaw. "If the trauma of all of this didn't trigger my memories, I might never get them all back."

He studied her for any signs as to how she felt

about that. She didn't seem upset. "Are you okay with that?" he asked.

Hanna nodded and gave him another of those dazzling smiles. "Maybe we can make some new memories," she said.

Jesse gave that smile right back to her and pulled Evan and her snugly into his arms. Yes, he was all for making lots and lots of new memories with Hanna and their son.

* * * * *

Look for more titles in USA TODAY *bestselling author Delores Fossen's miniseries Silver Creek Lawmen: Second Generation when* Maverick Detective Dad *goes on sale next month!*

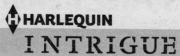
#2157 MAVERICK DETECTIVE DAD
Silver Creek Lawmen: Second Generation • by Delores Fossen
When Detective Noah Ryland and Everly Monroe's tragic pasts make them
targets of a vigilante killer, they team up to protect her young daughter and
stop the murders. But soon their investigation unleashes a series of vicious
attacks...along with reigniting the old heat between them.

#2158 MURDER AT SUNSET ROCK
Lookout Mountain Mysteries • by Debra Webb
A ransacked house suggests that Olivia Ballard's grandfather's death was
no mere accident. Deputy Detective Huck Monroe vows to help her uncover
the truth. But as dark secrets surrounding Olivia's family are exposed, she'll
have to trust the man who broke her heart to stay alive.

#2159 SHROUDED IN THE SMOKIES
A Tennessee Cold Case Story • by Lena Diaz
Former detective Adam Trent is stunned to learn his cold case victim is
alive. But Skylar Montgomery is still very much in danger—and desperate for
Adam's help. Their investigation leads them to one of Chattanooga's most
powerful families...and a vicious web of mystery, intrigue and murder.

#2160 TEXAS BODYGUARD: WESTON
San Antonio Security • by Janie Crouch
Security Specialist Weston Patterson risks everything to keep his charges
safe. But protecting wealthy Kayleigh Delacruz is his biggest challenge yet.
She doesn't want a bodyguard. But as the kidnapping threat grows, she'll do
anything—even trust Weston's expertise—to survive.

#2161 DIGGING DEEPER
by Amanda Stevens
When Thora Graham awakens inside a coffin-like box with no memory
of how she got there, Deputy Police Chief Will Dresden, the man she left
fifteen years ago, follows the clues to save her life. Their twisted reunion
becomes a race against time to stop a serial killer's vengeful scheme.

#2162 K-9 HUNTER
by Cassie Miles
Piper Comstock and her dog, Izzy, live a solitary, peaceful life. Until her best
friend is targeted by an assassin. US Marshal Gavin McQueen knows the
truth— a witness in protection is compromised. It's dangerous to recruit a
civilian to help with the investigation. But is the danger to Piper's life...or
Gavin's heart?

Get 3 FREE REWARDS!

We'll send you 2 FREE Books <u>plus</u> a FREE Mystery Gift.

FREE Value Over **$20**

Both the **Harlequin Intrigue®** and **Harlequin® Romantic Suspense** series
feature compelling novels filled with heart-racing action-packed romance
that will keep you on the edge of your seat.

HARLEQUIN
PLUS

Try the best multimedia subscription service for romance readers like you!

Read, Watch and Play.

Experience the easiest way to get the romance content you crave.

Start your **FREE TRIAL** at
<u>www.harlequinplus.com/freetrial</u>.